Dear Deborah
Enjoy!
I did.

Stella R.
xx
January 13, 2012

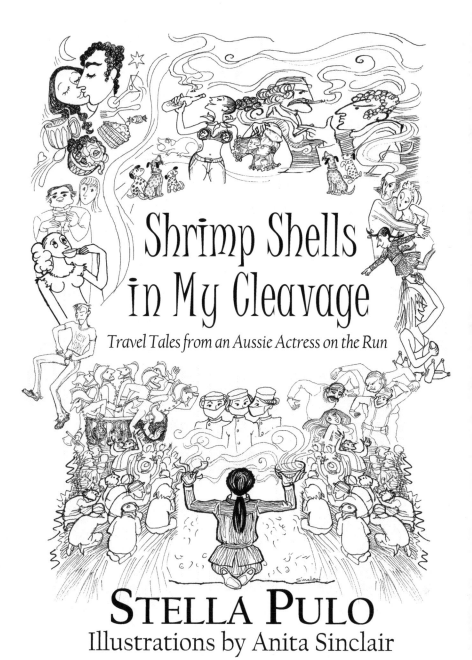

# Shrimp Shells in My Cleavage

*Travel Tales from an Aussie Actress on the Run*

# STELLA PULO

Illustrations by Anita Sinclair

*Foreword by Estelle Parsons*

For my father, Mr. George Pulo,
a true gentleman.
June 14, 1921 - May 10, 2007.
Dad, there's a chair at Covent Gardens
with your name on it.
Don't worry. I haven't forgotten.

# Contents

# Acknowledgments

To all the people who've encouraged me by laughing out loud and clapping a lot. There's been a ton of them. If I were to thank each as fully as they deserve, I would have to publish another book and, quite frankly, this one has taken long enough. Everyone has had something wonderful to offer. However, I would be remiss to not make very special mention of the following family, friends and colleagues who have swum along patiently with me and my *Shrimp Shells* ... making sure that I didn't drown along the way.

First and foremost, I thank my parents, George and Yvonne Pulo. I inherited my father's zest for traveling and my mother's appreciation for everything eccentric. I feel their love and support no matter how far apart we are from one another.

I wouldn't be holding *Shrimp Shells* ... in my hand if it weren't for Anita Sinclair, David Cady and Mary Fassino.

Anita Sinclair initially produced me in a storytelling event at her theater in Melbourne, Australia, and then kept presenting me with illustrations to entice me into getting my stories published. And entice me she did! Her talent, support, wisdom and tenacity spurred me on. I wouldn't love my *Shrimp Shells* ... as much as I do if it weren't for Anita Sinclair.

David Cady provided the perfect mix of all things that an artist cherishes: respect, sensitivity and expertise, belief in me and my work, and the patience of an elephant. He listened for hours, weeks and months, as I processed ideas, made decisions, and then changed my mind, again ... and again. I appreciate David Cady more than I could ever express.

And then came Mary Fassino with her

multiple array of talents. She was there at the precise time that I needed a design consultant. I am so very grateful to Mary for her time, insight and generosity. Mary Fassino proved to be the perfect person to help me put it all together, beautifully and creatively.

The support of Anita, David and Mary is between every line and on every page. I am forever indebted to them. They each respected my voice and never spoke louder than I did.

Thank you to Andrew Holden who, as Chief Editor of Melbourne Express (The Age, Melbourne, Australia), let me know what he thought of me as a writer by giving me my own column, SPNY. My gratitude is endless.

Thank you to audio and recording engineer, Mike Westbrook, for his time, patience and kindness, and for helping me to lift my stories off the page. Without Mike, I wouldn't have an audio book of Shrimp Shells ...

Thank you to Julia Gardiner who provided invaluable editorial assistance. To Marcia Haufrecht, who has always encouraged the storyteller in me and put her money where her mouth is by producing my work. To Richard Gaffield-Knight and the Red Harlem Readers, and Chander at the Indian Cafe, for the opportunities they provide to actors and writers. To Woody Regan and his workshop participants who are always there, loaded with talent and grace. To Edward Pomerantz and the Harlem Arts Alliance Dramatic Writing Academy. To Liz and Lloyd Jones of La Mama Theatre, Melbourne, Australia. To Susan Kirby, Jeffrey Hornstein, Tom O'Shaughnessy, Fran Madigan, Sharon O'Neill, Alphie McCourt, Jill Deeks, Betty Lou Holland, Genevieve Dinouart, Lynn McCann, Ellen Gibney, Jessica Slote, Mary Sayers, Damien Hewitt, Pushpa Ellis, Jonathan Eatmon, Keith Shinberg, Sue Henderson, Johnny Green, Chuck Japely and Josie Gaylor.

Thank you to The Actors Studio for reminding me to always strive for excellence.

A very special thank you to Estelle Parsons who has honored me and blessed my *Shrimp Shells* ... by writing the Foreword.

# Foreword

I love to read women's adventures: scaling high peaks of the Himalayas, encountering grizzly bears in Alaska, solo wilderness canoeing, plunging into the jungle to find primitive tribes ... But Stella Pulo has discovered another kind of women's adventure: encountering the denizens of the western world, observing their frustrations, their inexplicable behavior and making no judgments about the obstacles they present but adjusting to them just as other adventurers adjust to what nature in all her wildness presents.

I met Stella after seeing her work in Actors Studio sessions in New York City, tackling with gusto and an open mind challenges that other actresses might think twice about before jumping in. She brings that same wonderful down under spirit to this group of encounters. They are here to enjoy.

Estelle Parsons
New York City, 2011

# Introduction

I t all began from behind a white plastic desk in the ladies' bathroom of AXIS, a discotheque in Malta. I had gone to Malta to check out my roots and to kill some time before returning to New York for my final audition at The Actors Studio. From 4 p.m. to 4 a.m. my job at AXIS was to make sure that no one smoked in the cubicles, went there in pairs or dropped dead from heat exhaustion.

Prior to Malta I had been hopscotching from one place to another, taking notes of things that amused me and jotting these down on whatever was at hand: bar coasters, menus, backs of re-

ceipts, used envelopes, travel brochures, maps
... I ended up with a bag full of bits and pieces
and hoped that what amused me might also
amuse others. I thought that one day I would
transform these bits and pieces into something
else. I wasn't sure what: a one woman show, a
book of pics and poems, a photo journalism
piece ...

At AXIS the music was so loud that the
vibrations often made the toilet bowls crack. I
was sometimes able to have a conversation, but
not often. And since I couldn't hear anyone
speak, and my body language only got me into
trouble, I decided to sit there for twelve hours
a night marrying my memories and my notes. It
was from behind that white plastic desk that
*Shrimp Shells in My Cleavage* emerged. And so,
whether you're in a bathroom, on a bus or at the
beach, in Brooklyn, Bali or Bombay, come along
and hopscotch with me.

# I Love Paris ...
# No Matter How

When I was offered the opportunity of performing in Paris I thought it was too good to be true. I love Paris. In the end, everyone does. The cafes full of Parisians creating melodies with their speech. The cobblestone streets that tell tales of history. The architecture, so magnificent that you wish for it to engulf you as you walk past. Any criticism of France, its bureaucracy and its bombs, its people and their cruelty toward frogs, is soon forgotten while climbing the Eiffel Tower or strolling along the Champs-Élysées. Boarding a *bateau mouche* at Pont Neuf for a casual trip

down the Seine at midnight is guaranteed to put you in a state of Nirvana. With a glass of Beaujolais you toast the Notre Dame, the Louvre, the Conciergerie and the palaces along the way. You see the Obelisque de Luxor at Place de la Concorde where King Louis XVI had his head chopped off. *"Je suis perdu!"* he yelled. Well, he might have felt lost, but with a view like this, you don't. You imagine your head being chopped off. You don't complain as long as you can keep your eyes open until the last moment. The Île Saint-Louis is now on your left. You couldn't care less if a bomb dropped or if the Seine lay on a major fault line. This is the stuff that whizzed through my head as I eagerly said "Yes!" to performing in Paris.

With a complete show packed in two suitcases and loaded onto a trolley, I arrived at Porte de la Villette. With that much gear I looked like trouble. No taxi driver could be bothered with me. Some even abused me for asking and so ... Paris Metro, here I come.

With a shoulder bag entangled around my

neck, the trolley dragging behind me, and a Paris street directory clasped in my sweaty, cramped hand, I arrived at my "provided accommodation."

"My God!" I yelled.

Simultaneously, I heard, *"Mon Dieu!"*

Was I being chastised for not speaking French? No. Behind me was a fellow who was also loaded with gear. We had arrived at the same time, and he was as surprised as I was. His name was Jean-Pierre, and he was from Belgium. We were going to work at the same theater. We were also going to share the same living space: a totally gutted warehouse in one of the red-light districts of Paris, Rue Saint-Denis. This was the theater management's understanding of providing accommodation in the heart of "Grand Paris." Well, it had sounded good over the phone.

As we entered the warehouse we stumbled over a box of candles. Ah! This is for when we blow a fuse. Wrong! There's no electricity! We soon realized that there weren't any windows either. And so for five weeks, while living in the center of Grand Paris, candles were our only source of light.

Jean-Pierre knew very little English, and I knew even less French. We agreed from the start that a sense of humor was going to be a must. With dictionaries, laughter, moans and groans, we managed to keep sane.

Jean-Pierre had spiked red hair and youthful freckles. During heated conversations he'd punctuate his outcries by ripping off a hangnail and spitting it into the air. As it landed onto the ground he'd stomp on it with his huge yellow sneaker. If he didn't manage to synchronize the two actions he'd rip off another piece of finger and try again.

I first experienced this ritual when Jean-Pierre discovered that we had no bathing facilities. With bits of finger flying into the air and his yellow sneaker stomping rhythmically, he tried to explain that in his show he plays Vincent Van Gogh. During a dream sequence he has an affair with the devil. Sometimes he feels the impulse to smother his face with green and red paint.

Without ripping off my hangnails, I tried to explain that my situation wasn't any better. I played a homeless woman, Daisy Belle, and for my performance my hair is sprayed black and silver and I'm covered in mud. What were we going to do? There was a tap in the warehouse that produced water so hot that we used it to make tea. The only cold water outlet was the toilet cistern. Jean-Pierre had an idea.

I followed him into the streets, and from amid the *haute couture* sexy lingerie boutiques, condom vending machines and The Little Saigon Vietnamese Restaurant, we began to collect empty Vittel plastic bottles. Forty of them! Oh, I get it. We're going to fill these with boiling water before we go on stage and by the time we get off the water will be cool enough to throw over ourselves.

"*Oui, oui,*" responded Jean-Pierre excitedly.

Believe me, this wasn't the kind of shower that made you want to sing love songs!

The "kitchen" referred to in our contract consisted of a Bunsen burner, which sat on top of a wooden fruit crate, and two chairs. In the "bedroom" there were three cushions that I transformed into a mattress. Jean-Pierre was double my height. Nevertheless, he only had four cushions. This room had unsealed wall vents and faced the busy Rue Saint-Denis. We slept to the sounds of seduction, the buying and selling of bodies in the streets below. Sometimes we'd wake up covered in bits of plaster that had fallen from the ceiling during the night. Each morning we felt as if we had hangovers because, while we slept, we had been inhaling gasoline fumes that had seeped in from the street through the open-air vents and into our sleeping area.

Jean-Pierre, being the perpetual optimist, suggested that we *use* this situation creatively. After all, Van Gogh went crazy and Daisy Belle is homeless. Oh yeah! True artists at work here! Stanislavski would've sat up in his grave and applauded.

Despite our agreement to keep sane, Jean-Pierre's sense of humor wavered at times. He often threatened to follow in Vincent's footsteps and cut off his left ear if our living conditions didn't improve. I was prepared to put up with

anything if it meant that I could stay in Paris and do things like cruise the Seine at midnight.

Jean-Pierre and I realized that any complaints we had would fall upon deaf ears. The management consisted of Maurice, a frustrated director who pretended he couldn't speak English. He arrogantly maintained that he could only partially understand Jean-Pierre because he was from Belgium where they didn't speak *the real Français.* A great way to avoid complaints!

Maurice often wore red because, he claimed, it made him feel "revolutionary." Once, I spotted Jean-Pierre and Maurice walking hurriedly along the street. Jean-Pierre was still wearing his yellow sneakers and the red tracksuit that he had slept in the night before. Together they resembled the Russian flag swaying in the wind, unsure of which direction to take. For Jean-Pierre that decision was becoming clearer and clearer. Belgium!

We were warned that a speech teacher rented part of our "loft" at nine o'clock on Monday mornings. We didn't think that anything could

be worse to wake up to than the gasoline fumes
and the plaster falling on top of us, but we were
wrong.

The speech teacher was middle-aged, cranky,
and forever wiping the sweat from her brow
with her bare forearm. How sweat managed to
ooze from her face was beyond me. She wore
heavy pancake make-up, the wrong shade of
course, and hot pink rouge. These combined like
putty, blocking the pores of her skin and the
crevices around her chin, mouth and nose. Her

facial hair was also coated pink. You expected a cloud of pink dust to form whenever she raised an eyebrow or moved her lips to speak, but it all weighed too much to go anywhere. Somehow I couldn't imagine her seated on a bench at the Tuileries gardens or by a waterfall at the Bois de Bologne enjoying a beautiful, romantic spring afternoon with a French lover nibbling at her ear lobes. He'd probably get a mouthful of the pink stuff because she often forgot to stop at her jaw and made up her ears as well. We nick-named her Menopausa. She was a true example of mutton dressed as lamb. She wheeled a baby stroller instead of a shopping trolley. In the baby stroller, and lost among a bunch of baguettes, was her pet poodle dressed in designer baby clothes.

Paris is made up of about ten million old ladies with poodles, and Menopausa was no exception. However, hers wasn't named Fifi. She named it Neige. Neige was white; so white, in fact, that you'd think it had been dropped into a bucket of bleach. It had lemon butterfly clips attached to its ears. These matched Menopausa's, whose long red and gray sausage curls were partially held up at her temples with similar clips. At a glance one could see that the wings of the butterflies had melted. She had obviously left her head, butterflies and all, under the hair dryer for too long.

Menopausa had a fairly fit muscular body, but somehow the skin around her neck, armpits, elbows and knees had become too big for her. Parts of her body moved up and down, over and around a short white pleated tennis skirt and a white tank top. Her lemon bobby socks were tucked into ancient beige tap shoes that were secured with frayed satin ribbon. Only God knows why she wore tap shoes, probably to make more noise than was necessary.

Apparently her life had fallen apart when year after year she was refused an audition for the famous *Folies Bergère* on Rue Richer, Montmartre. I guess the management never forgot her first effort. No, I have no idea how she performed, but I did hear rumors that she had rolled up with a résumé, photograph, and an abdomen that spelled seven months pregnant. I guess she thought that if it could work for Barbra Streisand in *Funny Girl* it could work for her.

Menopausa's students were always on time. So that they didn't stumble in the dark, they entered with candles already lit. They stood in straight lines and proceeded to take out pieces of gauze from their make-up purses, wallets or from their top pockets. These were what they wrapped around their tongues for the next hour and a half while Menopausa proceeded to beat a tambourine and yell the vowel sounds, "a, e, i, o, u." With tongues wrapped in gauze and stretched from here to kingdom come, the class repeated her.

Menopausa crept around monitoring their progress, sometimes munching on the end of a baguette. I'd be scared stiff that she would use it as a weapon and poke it down my throat if she felt dissatisfied with my vocalizing technique. Just as scary, however, was her other hand garbed in a gynecological glove, ready to demonstrate on some poor victim exactly how far one's mouth and tongue could stretch. With one hand gripping their tongues and the other holding candles above their heads, the class resembled a group of grotesque Statues of Liberty.

To promote my show I would often go to the main tourist spots in Paris. On wobbly wheels I dragged Daisy Belle's portable home, a cart full of junk. On top sat Daisy Belle's four imaginary troops, stuffed rabbits: Adolph, Rudolph, Sylvester and Jeremiah. I would sing and hand out fliers. I quickly learned that the French have a wonderful ability to suspend their disbelief. As I walked toward them to hand out the fliers they would hold their noses and throw coins into my cart to keep me away.

On one of these occasions I was outside No. 6 Place des Vosges, where Victor Hugo once lived, when I was approached by a policewoman who asked me for "*les papiers d'identité.*" She looked suspiciously at my rabbits. I'd pinned "war medals" onto their chests. I guess she was wondering in which war they had fought and, more importantly, on whose side. If she had looked more closely she would have realized that the medals were, in fact, washers from the hardware store attached to yellow, red and green ribbon. I dug deeply into the cart and pulled out my Australian passport. The policewoman opened the precious document, looked at me and then at my rabbits. What was she expecting to find? The four of them on the front page with Stella their mum?

"Ah!" she exclaimed. *"Comédienne! Comédienne!"*

Honestly, she'd have been less surprised if I'd pulled rabbits out of a hat. Passers-by stopped and giggled. They must have thought that I was the only bag lady in Europe who carried a passport. It's lucky I did, because this turned out to be great publicity. Meet the real *Misèrable*, right outside Vic's bedroom.

Jean-Pierre decided that going insane, even if Van Gogh did, wasn't worth the trouble. Some mornings I would find him asleep in the kitchen, his head resting on the fruit crate in the same position it had fallen the night before, left ear still intact. (I had decided to hide all the knives long ago.) The title of my show, *Every Night Something Awful!*, had become more and more ironic as time went by and Paris became more and more beautiful. I simply did what Marie Antoinette had suggested the hungry peasants do, and ate cake, lots of it.

# Will the Real *Dolce Vita* Please Stand Up

They would've thrown each other into the River Arno had they both not weighed so much. Three weeks of pizza, pasta, pistachio gelato and McDonald's hamburgers had taken its toll. Besides, the River Arno is supposed to be one of the most romantic stretches in Florence. Too bad. On this particular night there was nothing romantic about it whatsoever. Chuck and Candy, two middle-aged Americans from Idaho, were having a serious argument.

"What do you mean you don't want to stay until the end of our vacation? We've already paid for the hotel!" he yells.

"I can't. That's all. I already told you why," she yells back.

"Well, it just ain't good enough. You had weight issues before we got here."

"Yeah, but I've gotten even heavier since we've been in Italy!"

"Yeah, well the Italians don't eat like us."

"They don't do anything like us! And they're too friendly. Always touching you, even if they don't know you! They wave their hands all over the place when they talk. It's goddamn danger-ous."

Chuck is holding onto his ears. He doesn't want to hear any more. Candy simply keeps going.

"I mean, in this place they tell you what to eat when you're the one paying for it. Yesterday I asked for some Thousand Island dressing for my salad and the waitress tells me not to be stupid."

"Oh, she didn't mean to offend you, honey."

"A waitress calls me 'stupid' and you tell me she doesn't mean to offend me!"

"Look ...," he tries to explain.

"Look nothing. I just wanna go home," she wails.

Chuck was okay even if he *was* wearing a red, white and blue satin tracksuit, and an ash-blond toupée under a baseball cap. Candy was wearing creased baggy white linen shorts, and on her head she had a Statue of Liberty sun visor. Her T-shirt read, "Come to Idaho and Have Yourself a fine Potato." Of course, she wore Reeboks and white bobby socks. Chuck did too.

During her outburst with poor ole Chuck, Candy did two particularly strange things. The angrier she got, the more fiercely she tugged at the wrinkles around her eyes as if to remind him that upsets of this nature were aging. Then, as she grew even hotter under the collar, she reached into her pink canvas Velcro money belt and pulled out a battery-operated fan. When she switched it on, an American flag popped up and started to wave. What a sight! Chuck and Candy had attracted an audience, an audience who wished that they had remembered their cameras.

One couldn't help but feel a little sympathy for Chuck. At least he appreciated *la dolce vita*, which at first his wife suspected was an Italian beauty with whom he had become infatuated. The truth is that all Italians appreciate *la dolce vita*, which isn't simply a woman or a film, but a lifestyle that permits Giuseppe to close his pizzeria for a while because he's decided that it's time to enjoy an espresso with Cousin Manfredo.

Giuseppe greets Manfredo with a slap on the back that's so hard Manfredo goes flying. The beautiful Italian designer shoes that he's been repairing fall out of his hands and knock over a jar of glue, which spills onto his workbench. Manfredo screams and yells, and somewhere amid the noise and commotion we hear, *"Come sta? Come sta? Bene. Bene."* The glue is left to dry in exactly the same place it landed. The Italian designer shoes are trampled on as Manfredo and Giuseppe exit to have coffee together at Luigi's cafe on the Ponte Vecchio. Anyone in Manfredo's shop at the time is ordered out and told to come back later. When? Later. That's all.

I was told that Luigi on the Ponte Vecchio made the best coffee in Florence. I visited him often. He nicknamed me *Cangura* (kangaroo) because I was from Australia. Luigi couldn't understand why Australia has kangaroos but Italy doesn't.

One day I heard Luigi calling me from across the street, *"Cangura. Cangura."* He was gesturing

excitedly for me to come to him. He closed the
door of his cafe and put up a sign, "*Chiuso.*" With
his English vocabulary of about six words and
mine of about five, plus a dictionary, we were
able to communicate. Luigi was pleading that I
get him a baby kangaroo from Australia.

"Luigi, it's difficult to smuggle animals from
one country to another," I try to explain jovially.

"*No problema,*" he assures me. "It can hide in
the pocket. This is how they born. No? *Bambini*

in *mama's* pocket."

Luigi was dead serious.

"Luigi, kangaroos grow very big," I explain.

"Italy also very big," he assures me.

I could just imagine a kangaroo hopping around the Duomo, taking a rest every now and then at the Gates of Paradise.

"I can to tie him up like the *Cinese* do with the feet. Then he not get big," continues Luigi.

"Luigi, it's too cold in Italy in winter. It will die," I say.

"No. He not die," protests Luigi. "I will make the fire for him. He be my *amico*," says Luigi affectionately.

A small group of customers were hanging around outside the door waiting for Luigi to re-open, but for Luigi, his obsession with kangaroos was far more important than business. He was horrified when I informed him that some people go kangaroo hunting and sell the meat for pet food. I jokingly suggested that he be the first in Italy to serve kangaroo meat pasta. This went over like a lead balloon. He cooked me a wonderful meal, which I was only allowed to eat after I taught him to hop like a kangaroo. Luigi now has two claims to fame. He makes the best coffee in Florence and can hop to your table without spilling a drop.

While in Italy I had the good fortune of meeting many marvelous cooks like Luigi, and all the food I savored was fit for a king. In fact, apart from Candy, I've never heard anyone complain about the cuisine in Italy. Even the cooks at McDonald's break a few rules as they bless the humble hamburger with that special Italian touch.

One day while sitting and enjoying a *pizza prosciutto e funghi* at Piazza della Signoria, I observed a young couple strolling hand in hand, both speaking at once. Suddenly the young woman slapped her boyfriend about the ears. He had obviously disagreed with something she'd said. Rubbing his ears he kept walking at the pace she had set, continuing to justify his argument. After all, what's a slap between lovers? Within minutes that same couple began kissing passionately. Next? Pizza and vino before going home to make love. There would be no thought of having to get to sleep early because of work in the morning. Life just isn't for that. It's for living. It's for family, friends, church, vacations and whatever else is in the Italian cultural repertoire of enjoyable things to do together.

The Italians I met didn't seem to be fussed about privacy, or the need for "personal space." No arm's distance apart. This means that one occasionally gets told off or gets one's ears slapped in public. But that's nothing. Just letting each other know what's what. Everything is loud and clear and straight to the point. No heart attacks or ulcers from stress and anxiety. Italians would rather die from other things. There's no such concept as too much of a good thing. If it's not good and plentiful, it's not welcome. For me, Italy is very different from everywhere else and, for Italians, everywhere else doesn't matter anyway. The best of everything is in their own backyard ... everything, except for efficient firemen, policemen and locksmiths. If you lock yourself out of your apartment anywhere in Italy, you're bound to meet all three parties and, perhaps, still be locked out a week later.

One afternoon I discovered that I had done exactly that, and the chief of the Florence Fire Department thought he would use my mis-fortune as a training session for his twenty newly recruited firemen.

To my surprise, the chief spoke to me in English. He informed me that the reason he could speak English was because he had to deal with many foreigners who always "go outside and leave their keys inside." He expressed his frustration by hitting his bald head rather savagely with the palm of his hand and stereotypically yelling, "*Mama mia.*" Then, as if petitioning God in heaven, he began wailing for mercy. He proceeded to explain that his "boys" were on their way. Each of them was going to be allowed a maximum period of sixty seconds to climb up the building and into my

apartment. He suggested that I watch, as the exercise could prove interesting. Great! I was about to be the guinea pig for the Florence Fire Department.

Soon the sirens of five fire trucks were heard throughout Florence. Lights flashed and everyone on Via dei Neri, the street on which I lived, was hysterical. With this much commotion, there must be a huge fire. Why else would five fire trucks and twenty firemen descend on the scene? My Italian vocabulary and dictionary weren't enough to explain that I had simply locked my keys inside my apartment and they had come to let me in. Neither would the chief explain the situation to the rapidly growing crowd. He thought it would be good practice for his boys to deal with a panic-stricken public.

It was getting chilly, so I asked the chief if the first fireman could let me into my apartment while the rest continued the drill.

"*No problema. No problema*," says the chief as he gently moves me aside but nowhere near the door to my building. It was clear that I wasn't going to get into my apartment before the drill was complete.

Every car wanting to travel through Via dei Neri is ordered to detour while twenty strong Italian firemen enter my apartment. The chief encourages the "audience" to applaud when any of the firemen take less than sixty seconds to complete the exercise. I remind the chief that the last fireman ought to leave the door open, for I suspected that he had forgotten the reason I requested his visit in the first place.

"*Prego. Prego*," he answers.

He then informed me that he had to see my rental contract before he could let me into my apartment.

"No problem. It's inside."

"No good inside. I must to see it here, outside, or I not to let you in, or the landlord he must to tell me that you are the tenant," he says assertively.

"I don't carry the rental contract in my bag in case I'm robbed, and my landlord lives in France."

"*Scusi. Scusi*," he says. "How I to know that this is your apartment?"

Unfortunately, he made sense, especially when he told me that in Italy, when tenants don't pay their rent, landlords make sure they don't get into their apartments by deliberately changing the locks on the doors. The situation proved impossible. Twenty firemen had just entered my apartment, but I was to remain locked out. I stood helplessly as I watched the Florence Fire Department proudly drive away and everyone else depart for their warm houses.

It was lucky for me that a man witnessing the event approached me and took me to meet his friend Roberto. Roberto displayed a bag full of keys and, for a bag full of money, he found the one that opened my door.

I love Italy. Everything gets done in its own time. Putting up a fight doesn't work. Give in or get out. Most foreigners give in because it's less frustrating and there's so much to gain that the compromise is usually well worth it. Some, like Chuck and Candy, get out with

31

nothing more to tell friends over dinner back home in Idaho than boring stories of frustration. Their loss. Italy doesn't care. What happens outside of Italy is none of its business.

# Just What I Needed: *Neighbours* on Top of Gastroenteristis

Getting sick in a foreign country can be scary. Despite how understanding you try to be, making comparisons between doctors, treatments and standards of hygiene is inevitable. You want the surgery, clinic or hospital you're visiting to look as similar as possible to the ones you go to in your home country. You know you're being a baby but you excuse yourself. You're sick. You're allowed to be vulnerable and pathetic. You may notice differences that have nothing to do with doctors' expertise, such as walls in need of painting, or magazines with the front page missing sitting on top of scratched coffee tables. You don't remember walls, magazines or coffee tables back home in such bad condition, and you hope that these aren't indicative of the professional standard you're about to experience.

You don't care who's recommended the doctor you're about to see or how many certificates he has plastered on his wall. Will he know what's wrong with you? Will he be able to tell you in English? And, most importantly, will he give you the right medication? You hope so, because you can't live another day with the stomach bug you've caught. If this doctor can't help you, you're going to catch the next plane home.

Now, I highly respect my stomach for its tenacity and ability to remain in one piece considering the stuff I sometimes put into it. In Italy I pushed it to the limit. I think everyone does when visiting Italy. My bowels objected violently. It served me right, but it was worth it. I found myself on a wild goose chase trying to find an English speaking gastroenterologist.

I learned of one who had studied in London and immediately made an appointment to see him.

I wait for two hours. Finally, he opens his office door, ushers a female patient out and invites me in. He is wearing a white cotton coat that is so creased it looks like it's just come out of the dryer. His slip-on shoes are dreadfully out of shape, split at the back, and in need of a clean and polish. Worst of all, he smells of cigarettes. I am trying desperately to stay positive. After all, getting rid of my crippling stomach bug is all that matters, and if he can do the job, great.

"Come in. Come in," he says. "You are the foreigner from Australia, ha? Very good. I need for to practice my English. *Scusi* if I am little red in my face but that woman you just see, she tell me that she have too many *problema* being woman. She come here every week. Every time same. So I tell her that maybe she want to change from being a woman to being a man and that we can do the operation for this. And she get upset with me! She pay for me to tell her what I think but then she get upset. I can never to understand womens. But *scusi*. How can I to help you," he asks, finally.

"I want a sex change," I say, testing his comprehension and his sense of humor.

At first he looks dismayed but then, when he realizes what I'm up to, he begins laughing.

"You must to be a comedian. What is your job?" he asks, as he flips through my patient data sheet.

"Ah! Actress. Actress. And you must to play the comedy, yes? You write the comedy also?"

"Yes," I answer.

"Oh, I must for to be careful, eh, in case you write something about me," he teases.

"Oh no! I wouldn't do that," I say, reassuringly.

"Tell me what it is like to be on the stage. You must to love when the people put the hands together? And then, when you go off of the stage, they still put hands together without stop so that you must to come back. Feel good, eh?"

I'm not sure if he's asking a question or being a frustrated actor, but he's getting very excited.

"Not at the moment, it wouldn't feel good. I'd be in too much of a hurry to get to the toilet," I respond.

I am trying to change the subject to the one I have waited two hours to discuss.

"So bad, eh? What's the matter for you?" he asks.

"I have very bad stomach cramps. My stomach feels like it's going to explode. You know. Boom. Boom. Hiroshima. Nagasaki," I explain.

"Ah! *Si, si.*"

"I have to run to the toilet. Very often. Very quickly. Maybe I'm eating too much pasta and pizza."

I try to make light of my condition.

"Never can to eat too much pasta and pizza," he says defensively.

"I tell you what, Doctor," I start to say.

"Please. You to call me Nazarino. Nazarino! Good actor name. You think so?" he asks.

"Ah, yes. Of course. I tell you what, Nazarino. I'll put my hands together for you very loudly. I won't stop. I promise. All of Italy will hear me. Just fix my stomach, okay?"

"You will to do this for me? That will be real great," he says, joyfully.

He instructs me to take off all my clothes, except for my underpants, bra and socks. Somehow it doesn't feel right. It feels *safe* enough, but it just doesn't feel *right*. The atmosphere is too, too ... casual. However, I am desperate and prepared to do anything to get rid of my stomach bug.

As Nazarino approaches me, he starts roaring with laughter.

"What's the matter?" I demand.

"Your socks! Your socks! You are truly actress. I can see. I can see. Animal skin socks."

I am wearing leopard skin Lycra socks. If only that's all there is to being an actress! Nazarino gets down to business, poking around my stomach, abdomen and everything else in that vicinity. He suddenly becomes quiet

and I start to worry that there is something seriously wrong with me. But, no.

"Have you been in the television show *Neighbours*? It's from Australia. I love this television show. It is famous for long time in all of Europa. I can to get all of the old copies here in Italy and I can to watch them on the television. Again and again."

He giggles as he points at something under his desk. I stand up and peer in that direction. There is a television set by his feet! It occurs to me that perhaps this is the reason why he was so behind with appointments.

As if reading my mind, he says, "But this is not why I late tonight. And don't you to worry about your stomach. You have the gastroenteritis. And maybe you just be getting used to all our beautiful Italian food, eh? I give to you something. These tablets. You take as many as you want. You soon will be feeling okay and can to go back to the stage. And now you can to get dressed. But don't forget to come back. We must to finish to speak about *Neighbours* and especially about that *bella donna*, Kylie Minogue."

I try to tell him that Kylie is very different now than when she acted in *Neighbours*, but for a moment, Nazarino is away with the fairies and can't hear a thing. Quickly, in case he forgets, he hands me his business card.

"Please, you to give this to Kylie and you to tell her that I wait for when she come to Italy

and her stomach give her the *problema*."

Nazarino's bookshelves are lined with cheap chrome photograph frames. Some of these are heart-shaped and hinged together with a cute and smiley, teenage Kylie Minogue on one side, and Nazarino with his bride on the other. He lifts one of the frames to his heart, kisses the side Kylie's on and whispers, "I love her." Somehow, I feel that Kylie is more important than my stomach could ever be. He reaches over to his desk and grabs a piece of scrap paper and a pen.

"Please, you can to give me your signature for when you become famous? And no *problema* about the money. I not to charge you. If you friend of Kylie so you friend of me too."

# Getting Waxed

If you want to get rid of excess hair from your legs, chin, face, armpits, back or stomach, then waxing is an unbeatable method. Once you've waxed and the hair slowly grows back soft, fine and fair, you'll never want to use a razor, depilatory cream, tweezers, sandpaper or your Swiss army knife again. One shot with any of these will put you back at square one: short, itchy bristles. Your legs, and other parts, will have the texture of a man's beard. Ouch and yuck.

Waxing hurts like hell. They say you get used to it, but you never do. Do you shriek when you have to rip off a Band-Aid? Do you close your eyes tightly, grit your teeth and ask your mother to do it? For those of you who've never been waxed, imagine pieces of calico, about eight inches long and four inches wide, slapped on top of a thick, hot toffee-like substance that has been spread onto your limbs, or wherever. After a few seconds when all is set, the beautician grabs the calico from one corner, the way your mother grabs the Band-Aid, and with one quick sweep rips out the hair, which until now has been sitting peacefully, minding its own business. You're stunned for a minute as you see the surface of your skin transferred onto the calico. Soon, little bloody red dots pop up everywhere. The hair follicles are in total shock, but they'll soon get over it and go on producing more of the stuff. There's no stopping them. Unless you've got many dollars, a lot of time and patience, and an even greater tolerance for pain than is required when being waxed. Then you may consider electrolysis.

Some people can wax themselves; others

can't. I'm one of the latter. Pity. It's cheaper to wax yourself. My budget has to accommodate a waxing at least every four weeks in summer and every six weeks in winter.

Was it going to be possible to maintain professional waxing treatments while traveling overseas for as long as I was intending? Well, suffice to say, the disposable razor was often very tempting. I had to resist it the same way I have to resist pastrami on rye at Carnegie Deli on Seventh Avenue in New York. By the time I got to a beautician for a waxing, I was usually very hairy and often used as a demonstration model on whom students could practice their waxing technique. Such was the case in Barcelona, where I didn't pay a cent and I was probably the hairiest I'd ever been in my life.

Walking along La Rambla one afternoon, I'm handed a leaflet. A nearby salon is offering discounts on all beauty treatments. It's scorching hot, and I'm sick of wearing long sleeves and trousers to camouflage my furry limbs, so I decide to visit the salon.

After killing time eating paella and drinking some particularly strong Sangria at Plaza Reial, I'm feeling a little intoxicated. This is exactly how I need to feel, considering the beauticians at this little salon are beginners and don't show much talent in their chosen profession. Six students at a time practice on me, and there's still loads more hair for a second shot if they so desire. I didn't expect much from the students, but neither did I anticipate coming out of the salon black and blue from their bad waxing technique.

I became desperate for another waxing treatment when I was in the Czech Republic. It was dirt-cheap there. I was quoted the equivalent of three bucks, although the price doubled once the beautician saw me undressed and realized that a trim was necessary before the waxing. Then, out came the vacuum cleaner. Not an ordinary broom. Oh no. Not for this much fluff!

I stand there in my bra and knickers and wait patiently for my body to be rescued from its wooly layer. I'm ushered into a room without a bed. I get waxed standing up! It's very funny and requires a total lack of inhibition on both our parts.

I've heard of people catching cholera from visiting salons that use recycled wax. Well, whether the wax at this salon has been recycled or not, I'm not going to catch anything. The wax is boiling hot! I give a shriek. The beautician lets me know quick smart that she isn't going to put up with any nonsense. The shriek I gave was my first and last. The filthy look I got from her settled that. Mind you, for the price, I could hardly complain.

It's always a vulnerable feeling to anger a hairdresser who has your head of hair in one hand and a pair of scissors in the other. Upsetting a short-tempered Czech beautician holding a pot of boiling wax above your armpit isn't a good idea either. It was at times like this that images of the disposable razor flashed before my eyes.

The beautician is a great deal taller than I am. So, as instructed, I stretch my arms above my head to maintain my armpits at a height within her workable reach. On with the wax, off with the curls. Oh yes! *Curls* is right. After four months we weren't just dealing with a five o'clock shadow.

Okay. So, that's the armpits done. I start to wonder what she's going to ask me to do with my legs. I'm certainly not fit enough to stretch them over my head. Well, luckily, I don't have to. She places her wax pot on the floor, puts her

hands between my knees and spreads them so that I stand with my legs eighteen inches apart. (Now, I'm trying hard to tell the story as it was and not deliberately create provocative images. Just take it from me. There was nothing even slighting erotic about this event. It was inelegant, clumsy and made worse by the fact that my underwear didn't match.)

With my hands resting against the walls for balance, the beautician kneels at my feet and starts to slap wax onto my legs. This is the first time in ages that I've dared to lift my arms while not wearing long sleeves. If you ever see someone in summer with their arms glued to their sides you'll know why. They're probably as neurotic as I am about bushes in their armpits. Be kind. At the supermarket don't ask them to fetch something from the top shelf.

Within twenty minutes the Czech beautician is finished. Hairless, hardly missing the change from my wallet, and about half a pound lighter, I say, "Thank you," and as I go out, I notice her running to the telephone. She's probably going to have a few laughs with a girlfriend about her encounter with the furry foreigner of Prague.

The Japanese don't have hairy bodies. Japanese beauticians, when dealing with hairy foreigners, control themselves quite well, too. I lived in Japan for sixteen months and came to the conclusion that the Japanese would rather burn their chopsticks than be offensive. I'm still trying to figure out what happened in this particular aesthetic salon in Shinjuku, Tokyo.

Obviously business hasn't been good, because the six young beauticians employed in this salon are all occupied with menial tasks. One is shining nail polish bottles. Another is on her hands and knees picking up the odd speck of dust. I suddenly have the urge to walk to a mirror and mark it with fingerprints just to keep someone employed for another ten minutes.

The six young beauticians stand in line as I walk past them, queen-like, down a hallway and into a pretty room with pink and white cherry blossoms printed on the curtains, wallpaper and cushion covers. Well, looks can be deceiving. There is nothing gentle or pretty about the way my body is handled.

After a few moments of silence, the beauticians, feminine in every sense of the word, start undressing me, slowly and quietly, almost as if performing a tea ceremony. As my hairy flesh reveals itself, the giggling begins. Bloody foreigners! Why can't they be smooth like us Japanese!

Giggle, giggle, "Ooh." I start laughing at the sheer ridiculousness of it and to make things more comfortable all 'round, but this has the opposite effect. Silence falls and they begin conspiring. Soon I'm hoisted onto a bed. I'm quite capable of climbing onto it myself, but for some reason I'm not going to be allowed to do anything. I feel as if I'll do someone out of a job if I as much as scratch my own nose.

The big boss enters, takes one look at me and screams. The girls pacify her by guiding her hand over my thigh and down my leg, showing her

that my hair is very soft and isn't going to be too difficult to remove.

She soon calms down. The beauticians stand back, passing her strips of calico, holding the wax pot and satisfying her every whim. They're wearing white uniforms, and had they been wearing masks and gloves as well, I would've sworn I was in an operating theater. With each strip of calico the big boss gains confidence, until she's attacking my hair follicles like nobody's business. With tears of blood they plead for mercy.

It's common practice to apply a little baby oil after hair has been removed. It moisturizes the skin and dissolves sticky bits of leftover wax. Common sense tells you that sprinkling talc on top simply creates a greasy white paste. Well, this salon used Vaseline rather than baby oil. Twelve hands smothered with massive amounts of the stuff descend upon me. Talc is then sprinkled up and down my gooey body. I look like I've been dipped in batter. I'm stuck to whatever is lining the bed, but this doesn't

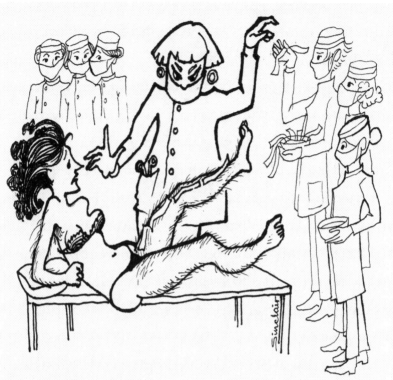

deter the young women from rolling me over. Feeling like a huge piece of tempura, I am tackled, and, on the count of three, "*ichi, ni, san,*" they flip me over. The Vaseline and talc routine is repeated up and down my back and neck, which are neither hairy nor have been waxed.

The beautiful Japanese beauticians manage to dress me, and as I wobble out of the salon, they each smile, thank me, bow (of course) and say, "*Sayonara*." The big boss isn't smiling. She's muttering, "Ueno."

In Ueno, a suburb of Tokyo, there's a beautiful park that has magnificent cherry blossom trees. In Ueno, there's also a zoo!

# Anything for a Buck

You end up with the weirdest jobs when you're traveling indefinitely and not fussed about what you do for a buck. The more alluring the country, the weirder the job. The hourly rate of pay is usually less than the change you carry in your pocket or what you might throw into a wishing well.

You justify your circumstances by telling yourself that any job will do, for the experience, for the money ... It's the only job paying cash in hand. It's the only job that's flexible, allowing you time to enjoy a new city. It's the only job going for someone like you, who could quit any

minute and continue traveling.

In Belgium, I tried door-to-door egg and potato selling, but gave up when I left a trail of egg white and dropped a bag of spuds along the sidewalk of one of the most prestigious streets in Brussels. The spuds rolled joyfully downhill, gaining pace as they went, thanking the good Lord for helping them to escape the nasty potato peeler.

In Berlin, I answered an advertisement for "sexy, husky voices." I had a strep throat at the time and thought I fitted the bill perfectly. Hank, a dirty old man, thought I did, too. He knew that in Germany there were many desperados, such as himself, and when they had nothing to do, and no chance in hell of a woman to do it with, they could dial the naughty number and listen to me telling them bedside stories in German. I had no idea what I was saying. This was of no importance to Hank. He simply concerned himself with correcting my pronunciation and instructing me to breathe heavily in between every two or three words. The departure of my strep throat and the return of my natural sounding voice marked the end of that career. Once, just for fun, I dialed the naughty number. My God! Is that what I sound like when I'm trying to be sexy?

In Macedonia, I got a cleaning job in a restaurant. Cleaning is usually pretty straight-forward. You don't have to think very much, thus preserving energy for more important issues. The quickest way out of this restaurant became an important issue for me when I learned that it wasn't only floors, doors, tables, sinks and toilets that I had to clean, but the inside of rabbits as well. Rabbits never stop bleeding! I began asking myself the same question you always ask when you hate your job. How badly do I need this? Well, I didn't know how to skin and clean rabbits, and now I do. Hip hip hooray! Come on. If you've skinned and cleaned a rabbit once, you've done it a million times. Well, I didn't skin and clean a million rabbits, but it soon felt like it.

It isn't easy to close a rabbit's eyes when it's dead, and they all seem to die with their eyes wide open. I would approach them wearing my starched white apron and carrying a twelve-inch dagger. We would look into each other's eyes, and I would apologize as quickly and sincerely as possible and then get on with it. I could never eat rabbit again, for I am now convinced that there's a conspiracy among them and they're out to get me. I must remember to keep my eyes open.

In Edinburgh, I didn't sell eggs and potatoes. Neither did I skin rabbits or tell bedtime stories in German. I dressed as a thirteenth-century princess and paraded through Edinburgh Castle handing out leaflets to tourists. I thought it would be fun putting on a Scottish accent and acting like royalty. Besides, I had always wanted to be a princess. However, this princess wasn't pale, pink and pretty like a Walt Disney princess. Instead, she was blue from the cold, shook uncontrollably and was clad in a football scarf and leather gloves!

Jean-Louis, an arrogant Frenchman who owned a nearby restaurant, told me that I didn't look the part and that I should come and work for him as a potato and garlic peeler. I soon decided that playing royalty and putting on a Scottish accent through chattering teeth was not my game. Mind you, neither was peeling potatoes and garlic for a quid an hour. Nevertheless, I approached Jean-Louis and reminded him of his offer. When he told me that I would be peeling potatoes and garlic, he wasn't joking. My day started with peeling a basket of each. Potato skin isn't kind on hands. Mine turned into sandpaper, and smelled so bad from the garlic that I spent my evenings soaking them in lemon juice to get rid of the smell.

The next stop was London, where I registered with a cleaning agency and was immediately sent out on a job. A newly renovated office block in Hammersmith was in a mess. Workers were still on site. Workers! Six hundred of them! All men! I was sure that God, Buddha and Germaine Greer were playing tricks on me. They could at least have spared me the embarrassment of wearing a helmet.

I hated the idea of wearing a protective helmet. If you saw my head and the size of my body, you would understand. I looked like a mushroom, and every time I tilted my neck, the mushroom got decapitated. Helmets are obviously designed for men, who have much bigger heads than women. I had hoped that by wearing a helmet I would appear less conspicuous. Not so. No matter what I do, I'll always look like a girl.

I had never been on a building site before, so I tried to make the best of things. What things! Not even separate bathrooms for men and women! The supervisor kindly handed me the keys to one of the newly renovated bathrooms in the building. The other alternative was the tiny portable *maisonette* (little house) used by the six hundred men. I happily accepted the supervisor's keys to a loo of my own.

However, there was no toilet paper in my private loo. Renovated, beautifully decorated in avocado green and apricot, but no toilet paper. And, the supervisor was nowhere to be found.

There was a heap of toilet paper in the little
house. I hid around the corner, peeping in every
now and then, hoping that it would become
vacant for a minute so that I could dash in there
and nick some of the precious stuff.

When I was certain that the little house was
vacant, I ran at full speed, dropping my helmet
along the way. Once inside, I snatched a huge
roll of paper and ran back to my loo as quickly
as possible, a huge white roll in one hand and a
huge white helmet in the other.

There were thirty-five floors in this building. Twenty of us were employed to clean the windows. Four thousand of them! Dobie, a South African man in his late twenties, was working on the same floor as I was. One of the best things about working junk jobs while you're traveling is that you meet tons of people roaming around the world and none are ever what they appear to be. Dobie was an exchange student, studying forensic anthropology. To make a few spare quid he worked as a cleaner, and when he felt extra broke, he allowed pharmaceutical companies to test drugs on him.

For six days each month Dobie would check out of his humble East End bed-sit and into one of London's top teaching hospitals. He would be ushered into a private room with a Jacuzzi. On the nearby antique chest of drawers would be an à la carte menu for that night's dinner and the following morning's breakfast. After six days Dobie marched out of the hospital rested, fed like a king, £600 wealthier, and with his arteries dilated, his blood detoxified and his liver and kidneys flushed and scrubbed. It didn't take long to convince me that being a guinea pig for a pharmaceutical company certainly beat industrial cleaning. Nevertheless, I didn't join the waiting list.

"Why don't you sell your eggs?" suggested Dobie.

"Do they have door-to-door egg sellers in London too?" I joked. "I did that in Brussels."

"No. You sell the eggs from your ovaries. Look," he said, as he handed me a newspaper article.

"Wanted. Compassionate, healthy woman to donate eggs (ova) for infertile couple. Confidentiality and anonymity assured. Medical procedure to be performed at teaching hospital in Central London. £1,500 compensation for your time and effort."

I must admit that I was really tempted. After all, I had been throwing away at least one egg a month, free of charge, since my early teens. However, I didn't join that list either. Nor did I return to the building site. I spent the next day nursing my aching neck, for the helmet was not only ridiculously large, but it was ridiculously heavy as well.

I soon scored a job in the busiest pub in the West End of London. I had never pulled a beer in my life. Nevertheless, in the evenings that's what I did. During the day I worked in the kitchen with Catherine, who was the manageress and cook of the pub and made Hitler seem like a nursery maid.

One day, out of the blue, as she was stuffing a piece of lamb with breadcrumbs, she turned to me and said, "Did you know that I have an irritable bowel?"

"No. I didn't," I replied.

I hoped for her sake that it wasn't as irritable as her temper, but it obviously was. Catherine's bowel had become so irritable that she had to hire a cook, Jim, to take her place. I immediately nicknamed him Rice Bubbles on account of his complexion. A worse acne-ridden face in the entire British Empire was yet to be found. I was never tempted to nibble in this kitchen. In any case, it was one of Catherine's conditions when she hired me that if caught doing so she would instruct McVittie, her Alsatian, to bite off my hands.

McVittie was forced to wear tartan boots that he really resented. I'm sure he would've preferred to have not had feet rather than have to wear those boots. I watched as McVittie the Alsatian pleaded with Catherine the Pit Bull to remove the stupid things. The more he objected, the harder she kissed his long pointed ears.

I never knew what mood to expect from Catherine or from Rice Bubbles. In the evenings he worked as a lighting technician in a striptease club in Soho, and if he liked the look of the girls on stage that night he was great in the kitchen the next day. If not, he was like a ticking bomb about to go off any minute.

It must have been while lighting these peep shows that Rice Bubbles concocted the menu for the pub. To my embarrassment, I had to serve dishes with names such as "Luscious Lily's Lamb

Fry," "Marvelous Mary's Meat and Potatoes" and "Ravishing Rhonda's Crispy Beef Balls." He once threw left over rice into a beef casserole and named the dish "Mince Meat and Maggots."

"Pork Madras" was his favorite, and he didn't nickname it anything. He spent hours cooking his "Pork Madras" and couldn't understand why people never ordered it. I could. If customers spot a cook covered in blood and curry with a face that resembles the Sahara Desert during a sandstorm, the last thing they'd want to eat would be pig, right? Snap, crackle, pop, vomit.

Rice Bubbles was a slob in the kitchen and difficult to look at, but I did like him. While the rest of the staff tried to wake themselves up in the morning by listening to heavy metal music, Rice Bubbles listened to Vivaldi through his headphones. He must have instructed his barber to design a haircut that facilitated the head-phones, for they knew exactly where to sit when he placed them on his head. Either this, or his hair had grown around them. Anyway, his head-phones never moved, and when he took them off,

Sinclair

he looked as if he still had them on.

London's one of those cities where there's always work if you speak English, need a quick buck and aren't fussy about what you do for it. At this pub there was Otto from Bulgaria, who was overweight and hairy. It was his job to get rid of everyone when the closing bell rang. When it came time for people to vacate the pub, he simply took off his shirt and started shaking his flab to whatever music was coming out of the jukebox. In an instant, people picked up their belongings and were gone. Many pints of Guinness and bottles of Sol were left untouched.

Alan was the head barman and a super hunk! But I couldn't understand a word he said. His Liverpuddlian accent was very very thick. He had to repeat everything at least twice before I got it. "Pardon? Eh? What did you say Alan?" So romantic! I resorted to gawking at him instead and hoped that soon he'd gawk back and then ask me to marry him.

I decided to stay in London and work with these crazies until Christmas. The staff party promised to be great fun and, for me, it certainly got off to a good start. Alan the Hunk came dressed as Santa Claus. This gave me the perfect opportunity to sit on his knee and to tell him what I wanted for Christmas. (Body language came in handy.) Rice Bubbles dropped by in between strip acts. He was dressed as a Christmas food basket. I didn't know what his head was meant to be, mixed nuts perhaps.

And Santa? That Liverpuddlian hunk in disguise? Well, he surprised me all right! But not with the Christmas present I'd hoped for, but with a confession! He had a wife, two kids and another on the way!

# Meet the Real Cinderella ... Me!

There was only one way to get to know that totally eccentric layer of people that I knew existed in New York, and that was by getting into their apartments. On my very first visit there I signed up with Butlers and Maids. This agency was run by Una and Mary, a couple of mad Irish strawberry-blonde twins in their seventies. If their clientele was anything like they were, I knew I'd get exactly what I was after, and I did, starting with the first job.

Stark naked she opens the door of her Queens apartment and stands there staring at me.

"Hello," I say nervously. "I'm Stella, from Butlers

and Maids."

"Don't mind me being naked," she says. "Knew they'd send a girl so I didn't bother getting dressed. Too hot! I'll put on a wig for you. How 'bout that? Come in! Come in! If you can! There's a lot of junk all over the place."

She wasn't joking.

The floor of the apartment wasn't visible: newspapers, junk mail, unopened and half opened packages, ring tops from soft drink cans, rusty razor blades, stamps torn from the corners of envelopes, dried bread crusts, half eaten boxes of chocolates covered in ants, stirrers from take out coffee, sachets of sugar, crumpled paper napkins that had been used to wipe off lolly pink lipstick, cigarettes butted into the carpet, and pills, tablets and cough syrup spilled from their bottles. The place was like a junkyard and smelled like one too.

"I need you to create a pathway so that Dick can wheel himself from the bedroom to the bathroom and back. Make sure all the garbage goes into the correct garbage bags. They're labeled and lined up along the kitchen wall. Sometimes when I get the urge, I start to pick things up but I can't bend for long. I gotta bad back."

"Why don't you put stuff straight into the garbage bags?" I ask.

"Because they're in the kitchen and I'm usually in here," she snaps. "Good enough answer?"

The floor felt like it was moving. Masses of well-fed cockroaches were playing hide and seek with the ants.

"You can vacuum most of them. The ones in my bed are dead. Everything in my bed always is. Tried to have a baby for years. Every time I went to bed with someone, in fact. Married one of 'em, Dick. Made no difference. He's like a baby anyway, except he's in a wheelchair, not a baby stroller. Pees in his pants. Had to get him diapers. A bit of a job, him getting used to peeing in his diapers n'all. But, I wasn't gonna have him pee all over the place just because he couldn't wheel himself to the bathroom on time, now was I? Have to send him away every now and then for some training. That's where he is now. At training. Don't know why his private parts are affected but they are. His seeds don't work anymore. Would still love to have a baby though."

She was over seventy but seemed to think that she still had "seeds" and that they could still work.

I put on my rubber gloves and started picking up the newspapers. This woman needed the Blessed Virgin to perform a miracle, not a cleaner, and I was in need of Mother Teresa's patience.

"But you never know," she continues, "he might surprise me one of these days. Trouble is, when I feel something moving in my bed, I give it a good hard hit 'cause I think it's a cockroach. I don't go for the rabbits, though. I know when it's them. They're gentle, soft and furry."

"Rabbits!" I exclaim in disbelief.

"Yes," she replies. "When we weren't having much luck in the baby game, we bought a couple of rabbits and let 'em run 'round. They're supposed to bring good luck. The man in the pet shop told us they were both boys. But they weren't!

That's why there's still rabbits here fifty years later."

"Where are they?" I ask.

"You'll see 'em," she assures me. "Wait 'til you start vacuuming. The noise gets to them. They start hopping around all over the place. By the way," she says, suddenly changing the subject, "my name's Dotty, but every time you call me 'Dolly' I'll throw you a quarter. That's how people make their tips around here. Grab that suitcase from under the couch, will you, dear? My wigs are in it."

While I picked up vintage pieces of garbage and vacuumed cockroaches and rabbit pellets, Dotty sat on a chair trying on a variety of Dolly Parton wigs.

"I tell you what. I'll call you 'Dolly' for the rest of the day and you don't have to tip me, but how about putting on some clothes?"

"Okay. I've got just the thing," she says, enthusiastically.

Out came a pink polka-dotted nightie from under the cushion on which she was sitting.

"Great," I say, with a sigh of relief, "Dolly Parton would love it."

"You think so? Oh, you're a good girl. Hope you're chucking out the trash properly. Gotta separate everything or I'll get a fine."

Apart from clearly labeling and separating her garbage bags, Dotty was totally disorganized and neurotic as hell. She blamed it on a fall that happened one day when she decided to take a bath and then couldn't lift herself out of the water. Dick was on one of his training sessions. Dotty was stuck in the bath for two days.

"I hate bathtubs," she says. "Don't even bother cleaning it. It don't deserve it. Anyway, it's out of bounds."

"Where do you wash?" I ask.

"I use the sink, but Dick has to go without 'til he gets to training. He can't reach the sink properly sitting in his wheelchair n'all. Spills water all over the place."

"Oh, that's terrible!" I exclaim.

"Terrible! I was stuck in a cold bath for two days! That's what was terrible! Couldn't get the doorman or security to come up, didn't matter how much I yelled. They couldn't hear me. Just had to flood the place 'til all the water leaked into the apartment downstairs. That got 'em up here quick smart. Pity I didn't think of it two days earlier. Are you done with the vacuuming?" she asks, suddenly changing the subject.

"Yes," I reply, not that anyone could ever be *done* with anything in that place. It had obviously never been cleaned since Dick and Dotty started living in it.

"Good. Now take this feather. Not against using animal products, are you? Not one of those animal rights pains-in-the-butt are you?" she demands. "You wouldn't wanna be. Not 'round here anyway. Sucking up all them living things into the vacuum cleaner n'all. I treat the rabbits okay though. Don't you think? They've got the whole apartment to run 'round freely in. Not even Dick can do that," she laughs.

"What do you want me to do with the feather?" I ask, dreading her reply.

"I want you to concentrate on the lamp-shades. There are six of 'em. They're all the same. Tiny, tiny pleats. Can't put the vacuum cleaner to 'em or the pleats'll come undone. So you have to use a feather. Look. I'll show you."

I was having a great deal of trouble taking this seriously. Dotty carefully balanced herself and began to demonstrate. As she struck the lampshade, the feather got stuck on a rusty staple that was holding the insect infested thing together. It tumbled off the table and onto the floor.

"Oh well. Can't win 'em all. But that's how you do it. You gotta get in between the pleats. By the way, you probably won't get time but if you do, I want you to dust my hands. I don't mean my own personal hands. I mean my sculptures."

I hadn't seen any sculptures.

"Come on. I'll show you," she says.

A door in the kitchen led to a damp and dingy room.

"These are my hands. You wouldn't believe that some of America's most famous people have

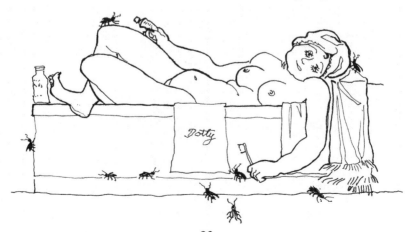

posed for me in here, would you? Here's a photo of me with Nureyev. God bless his hands. Anyway, if you get a minute, give everything a good hard dust. Don't lift any of them by the fingertips. They'll snap off. Especially Lillian Gish's. Oh! She had beautiful hands, smooth as porcelain. Fingertips like rose petals. I had beautiful hands too, once upon a time," she mutters as she leaves the room.

There were two shelves full of magnificent clay sculptures, the hands of various actors, dancers and musicians. She obviously liked strong, expressive hands, not only small, delicate ones. It took no effort whatsoever to imagine these in motion.

On the end of one of the shelves was a pair of very small, dainty hands, of a middle-aged woman perhaps. I blew the dust off from the attached label. Ah! "Blossom Dearie." Close by, another label read "Ray Charles." I couldn't decipher the names on some of the labels, for they were faded, discolored and specked with insect droppings. However, Rita Hayworth,

Cyd Charisse and Lena Horne had also posed for Dotty.

On the wall was a framed contract from a famous cosmetic company, dated 1958. Dotty had been commissioned to design a hand-shaped bath soap. Underneath the frame was a box of these, more than just the few one would expect to be kept as souvenirs or memorabilia. I suspect that once the soaps had been produced, Dotty couldn't bear the idea of her work melting away and passing through New York City's drainage system. She must have bought the lot. Some had crumbled into powder. The box of soaps had become a burial ground for dead mosquitoes, cockroaches and other bugs. There were many live ones too, disrespectfully nesting all over Dotty's fine work.

Every now and then I'd spot a photograph of a beautiful woman, also covered in dust and cobwebs and hidden behind the hands of Pavarotti, perhaps, or Bette Davis. This was Dotty, the woman sitting in the other room amid garbage, rabbits and roaches, and whose greatest joy was a stranger calling her "Dolly." This was Dotty when she was young and looking forward to having a family.

I realized that the lampshades weren't done, but they were in such a state that Dotty wouldn't have known whether I'd cleaned them or not. Besides, I'd mislaid the feather. I went into the living room. Dotty was sitting with her eyes closed, holding my red and black hand-knitted mohair coat that I'd bought in Malta. She opened her eyes, rested the coat on her lap and said, "Good strong hands knitted this. Someone with a very even temperament. It ain't tight in some places and loose in others. But don't worry. I don't want to keep it. You know, I don't like wearing clothes."

# Paprika, Pedicures and the Polgár Sisters

'm not sure why I went to Budapest, but I did. There was a train from Vienna, and I had the time and nowhere else in particular to go. Maybe I planned it in my last life while sucking on a paprika. I don't know. But there I was on my way to Budapest. I didn't know much about Hungary, except that the cuisine was reputed to be fabulous and that putting something into your mouth was like taking your palate on a picnic.

On the train sitting next to me was a sophis-ticated older gentleman named Janoo. He had told me his age before he told me his name. I

was meant to act surprised, so I did. It paid off, because from then on, I had a guide while vacationing in Budapest.

We were soon to arrive at Keleti Railway Station. The Hungarian passport control officers made it to our carriage just in time.

"My God!" I exclaim. "Look at the size of them!"

"It's all the paprika," whispers Janoo. "A Magyar maid was once haremed for the Sultan's pleasure during the time Hungary was occupied by the Turks. She escaped taking many paprika seeds with her and planted them all over Hungary. Smart woman! Paprika makes the men strong and the women beautiful. Hungarians love paprika. If you wear paprika around your neck it will keep away the bloodthirsty vampires and it will make you look better. Good for Hungary. Good for you."

"Right! I'll get some straight away," I reply, tongue-in-cheek.

Janoo was born in Hungary, educated in London and now lived in Belgium. He was a retired businessman who liked to keep his fingers in a few different pies. Little did I know that I was soon to be in one of them.

Janoo was excited that I was Australian as he considered Australian wine to be among the best in the world. I was sorry to inform him that he had chosen the wrong person with whom to have a conversation about wine. I'm not much of a wine connoisseur. My taste buds are in no way refined. I can happily drink Sauterne with a pepper steak. Janoo gave me a look of dismay when I told him this, but wasn't at all discouraged. He insisted that I accompany him to a "very special wine tasting" for which he had come to Hungary.

Now, I don't usually say yes to a date with a total stranger, especially for something like a wine tasting in the Hungarian mountains, but Janoo appeared safe enough and something told me that it would be fun.

We arrived at Keleti Railway Station. Janoo helped me get to my *pensione*, took my telephone number and bade me good night. He would soon be in touch to arrange a few outings, including, of course, the wine tasting. Before he left, Janoo made me promise that I would take a walk to the top of Gellért Hill first thing in the morning.

The best view of Budapest is from Gellért Hill, which one climbs via many steps and snaking paths. Gellért Hill is the setting for many famous legends. According to a German Danube legend, a beautiful Water Queen dared to disobey her husband, King Ingold, by joining a witches' feast on top of the hill. She was destined for Satan until good old Doctor Faustus came along and wrapped her in his cloak. No one knows who she ended up with, but Ingold must have been pretty boring for the Water Queen to prefer the company of a bunch of witches.

Halfway up the hill there's a monument dedicated to Bishop Gellért. The bishop shouldn't be confused with some of the men one is likely to meet along the way. These men pose as the bishop until tourists come near. Then, without further ado, they expose themselves. According to the Christian legend, the Swiss bishop was

nailed to a barrel and thrown into the Danube. Sadly, these guys aren't. Oh well! Obviously more interesting things happened on top of the hill in the old days than happen today. But, despite the few men who hang around up there and exhibit their wares, the view of Budapest from the top of the hill is indeed spectacular and the climb is definitely worthwhile.

The Hotel Gellért houses the magnificent Gellért baths founded by the Knights of St. John. Apparently these are the same baths where St. Elizabeth once treated lepers. None of the incidents involving the bishop, the

Water Queen, St. Elizabeth and the lepers or the flashers on the hill prevent the rich and famous from staying at the hotel and going in for a dip. Richard Nixon, the Shah of Persia and Raquel Welch, just to name a few, have enjoyed the baths, which offer remedies for everything from chronic nail biting to premature hair loss. Well, I certainly didn't leave looking like Raquel, that's for sure. Perhaps I should have worn a wreath of dry paprika around my neck as Janoo had suggested.

Despite the sheer elegance and brilliance of the hotel, the domes of colored glass, the mosaics, the pillars and the Hungarian Art Nouveau decor, some things, such as the pedicure salon, were hideously lacking in elegance. After walking around Europe for ten months, I decided that my feet could do with some serious attention, and here the best, apparently, was offered for five bucks plus tip.

The idea of putting on a pair of rubber flip-flops, slimy from sitting in a bucket of antiseptic all day, wasn't very inviting. However, this is what welcomed me as I entered the salon. There I was in one of the world's most grandiose hotels wearing slimy gray flip-flops.

Soon my name was called, and I flip-flopped and sloshed my way to a gray vinyl chair. Without any warning my feet were plunged into a gray plastic bucket, which also contained antiseptic. All buckets and chairs matched, though not all sets were gray. Perhaps they were color-coded. I was hoping that the gray sets were for sensitive feet, but I soon learned otherwise. Deciding that my feet had soaked long enough, the pedicurist took them out of the water and banged them onto her lap.

Someone tickling your feet is the worst form of torture, especially when you're at the Hotel Gellért and can't scream or laugh out loud. The pedicurist went straight for my tickle points and started to give them a rub. "Please" was one of the few words I knew in Hungarian and I said it over and over again, *"Tessék! Tessék!"* She interpreted my cries for her to stop as me pleading for more. Finally I screamed, *"Nein!"*

hoping that it meant "No" in Hungarian as it does in German. No such luck. However, I was successful in getting her to stop.

"*Nem, nem,*" she corrected me.

"Okay. Okay," I said. "*Tessék nem* on my feet or I'll ha ha ha to death."

Not liking me telling her what to do, she grabbed my ankles and yanked me forward so aggressively that I slid down the chair and almost landed with my butt in the bucket. With a magnifying glass she inspected my feet, which were now at her eye level. She moaned and groaned and reached for a very sharp primitive looking instrument. Did I hear right? Was she actually suggesting that I relax? Fat chance!

From the sweat on the pedicurist's brow, I gathered that my feet must have been hard work. I tipped her generously and set off on my merry way.

I arrived at my *pensione* to find a note from Janoo. He was going to pick me up the following morning for an excursion to the Budapest food market near Tolbuhin Körút. Afterward we were to go, by train, to the professional wine tasting that he had spoken of. Despite my declared lack of expertise as a wine connoisseur, he still insisted that I go where I knew I was destined to make a fool of myself.

Janoo had promised to buy his ninety-year-old mother some smoked venison. So this item is first on the shopping list. The food stalls en route to the venison get more and more grotesque as we move along. I don't know whether I'm feeling sick or hungry. Welcoming me to the breakfast table that morning had been two fat sausages, one black and the other white. The black sausage was made by stuffing the intestine of some animal with pig's blood and other things. The white one was made with liver, lemon and garlic. Of course, there was paprika on the table and strong black coffee. I had only had the coffee and am feeling hungry. However, nothing at this market is appetizing. Great! The wine expert from Australia, capable of getting drunk simply by sniffing the cork of a wine bottle, is going to sip Hungarian wine, buckets of it, on an empty stomach!

While Janoo deliberates over which blob of venison to purchase, I take a stroll through the live animal section where pigs are a feature. Little boys stand in groups, eating ice-cream, giggling and mimicking the pigs. Noisy electronic toys are nowhere to be found at this market, but there is a lot of other noise as Gorbachops and Zsa Zsa Gapork, the two fattest pigs, realize what's coming. Two kitchen hands from the renowned Kéhli restaurant and the equally renowned Gundel have just negotiated a deal with the pigs' owner. With rope around their necks, Gorbachops and Zsa Zsa are escorted away. Well, at least at the Kéhli and the Gundel, Gorbachops will enjoy the pomp and refinement that were missing while imprisoned in an iron pen. And Zsa Zsa, surrounded by a bunch of beautifully garnished vegetables smothered in fancy sauce, can finally enjoy being the center of attention.

Janoo catches up with me at the poultry stand and soon wishes he hadn't. Trying to

convince us of the freshness of her chicken, a woman draws us close, lifts one to our faces, and then expertly yanks its legs apart splitting it in half. Ouch! This sure embarrasses Janoo who looks at me, red-faced, and then proceeds to curse at the woman in Hungarian.

A little further on we see crates and crates of broken eggs. These are sold to the less affluent. They aren't merely cracked eggs; most are minus the shell or sitting in a piece of one.

Vendors sell everything at this market. Beyond the obscene poultry, broken eggs, armies of paprika, garlic and corn, is a row of Gypsy men from Transylvania holding their wives' underpants to their chests. Judging by how cheap these are, the Gypsy men don't think much of their wives. Poor Janoo! He's so easily embarrassed. First the chicken incident and now the underpants. I guess he's hoping I won't notice or ask questions, but there is one I have to ask.

"Janoo, who are the women whose faces are printed on the underpants?"

"They're the famous Polgár sisters of Budapest," he replies. "They defeated the Grandmasters at chess."

The Gypsy salesmen offer me "a good price," but although I'm short on underwear, I'm not tempted to buy any, even though I'm offered a free bra as a bonus. The salesmen throw the underwear onto the ground and start playing the cimbalom, a fabulous sounding instrument that we will still hear when we reach Vörösmarty tér from where our bus is soon to depart.

The idea of me being on a committee of professional wine tasters is too absurd for words. Janoo will hear no excuses. Australian wine is highly regarded in Europe and I come from Australia. That's all that matters to him.

The Hungarian countryside is very pretty and I'm taking a good look as I'm probably going to be too sloshed to see anything on the way back.

We reach the wine bottling plant, which appears to be ultra modern, and a tour of it, with Janoo in the role of interpreter, proves very interesting. As usual, looks can be deceiving. This plant may appear modern, but as we approach the area set aside for the wine tasting event, eight young women dressed in white are sitting in a circle on the bare concrete. Nearby are hundreds of wine bottles. These women spend ten hours a day, every day of their working lives, licking huge labels and then sticking them onto the bottles.

"Janoo," I ask, "surely in a wine plant as modern as this there'd be a machine for sticking labels onto bottles?"

"Not when there's unemployment," he replies.

I find myself sitting at an oblong table with loads of cheese and crackers and surrounded by men the size of mountains.

We introduce ourselves, and after I say my name, Janoo leads a discussion, in Hungarian, of course. I keep hearing "Australia. Australia." Oh God! Please don't let him be setting me up as some sort of expert.

Our task is to compare wine until we find those that, in our opinion, taste most like Belgium's most popular red and white wines. Janoo maintains that, unlike the French who will drink only French wine, the Belgians know what they like and will happily switch to cheaper wines that taste as good. Janoo's plan is to export to Belgium the Hungarian wines that taste most like the Belgians' favorites.

With no knowledge whatsoever of Belgian wines, blow me down if the wines I vote for aren't the two out of the forty-eight that are

chosen. Janoo is very proud of me when the announcement is made. If my friends could see me now! Janoo can't work out why I had deliberately tried to mislead him regarding my expertise. He puts it down to my being modest. On the way back from the wine tasting I have to answer Janoo's many questions about Australian vineyards. It's useless telling him that I've never been to one.

The image of those underpants with the print of the Polgár sisters plays havoc with my imagination. They'd make a good prop for some bent cabaret in my next life. Much to Janoo's disgust, I decide to return to the market and purchase a pair. Yes, I do get a free bra, though I'm somewhat disappointed with the face printed on it: one of the Gypsy salesmen!

With the Polgár sisters to keep me company, a wreath of paprika around my neck and my feet in good nick, I was soon to depart Budapest. Hungarian food did prove wonderful in the end, although I'd never recommend breakfast in Budapest.

# The Blessed Virgin and Her Secrets

With nowhere better to go, I boarded Bus No. 201 from the main terminal in Skopje, Macedonia, and headed toward Dubrovnik.

Whenever I arrive somewhere new, my normal routine is to find somewhere to live, visit the tourist office for maps and other bits of information, and then look for the building with the famous red, white and blue stripes: the American Express office.

I decide to stay with a Croatian family who are happy to rent the spare rooms in their house to tourists. I have one room and a family from

Western Australia has the other.

"What brings you here?" they ask.

"Oh, I'm just traveling 'round," I reply. "What about you?"

"We're here to visit the Blessed Virgin Mary in Medjugorje," they answer.

"Excuse me," I say, "I have to find the American Express office to change some money."

Blow me down if the American Express office in Starigrad wasn't busy selling a tour to "Magical, Mystical Medjugorje ... where the Blessed Virgin appears every night, and where unexplainable happenings occur." I thought that selling a religious tour was somewhat unconventional for American Express and was inspired to inquire further. The woman at the front desk was well versed on the topic and, as it turned out, a good salesperson too.

Apparently, in June of 1981, six children were tending sheep on the side of a hill. They looked up and saw a woman holding a baby. She was wearing a long blue gown and a crown, and looked radiant. The children ran home.

Those in total shock never returned. They probably never went anywhere else either. The others, the "seers" or "visionaries," Vitska, Maria, Ivanka, Mirijana, Ivan and Yakov, had been visited daily and told "secrets" by the Blessed Virgin, who referred to herself as the "Queen of Peace." There were ten secrets and each referred to wars and other world disasters that had happened, were about to happen or were happening at the time. Exactly what the secrets were, and how many had been told, was anyone's guess. So that the visionaries weren't accused of lying, the Blessed Virgin promised them that each time she shared a secret, a permanent sign would be left at Medjugorje, and in other places also.

The woman at the American Express office advises me not to go to Medjugorje on Mondays or Fridays.

"Why not?" I ask.

"Because," she explains, "the Blessed Virgin asked for fasting to be observed on those days of the week as an expression of people's love for her and to prevent more wars. Whether you agree or not, you don't get anything to eat or drink on Mondays or Fridays."

When the folks at American Express say you can't leave home without them, they know what they're talking about.

Curiosity got the better of me. Within a couple of days I found myself back at the American Express office buying a ticket for the two day tour of magical, mystical Medjugorje.

Medjugorje is set in the mountains of Herzegovina, about sixty-three miles east of Split and the same distance northwest of Dubrovnik.

When the bus on which I was traveling reached Medjugorje I couldn't help thinking that the Blessed Virgin could have picked a better place to appear. Then, when I realized that I was the only tourist among six hundred pilgrims, I thought that I could have picked a better place, too.

Medjugorje has to be one of the ugliest villages in Europe. There is virtually no vegetation.

The gray concrete houses blend with the gray sky, pebbles, mud and dirt. The only sign of color is the rainbow created by a mile of rosary beads which line the street leading to St. James Church, the church where the Blessed Virgin appeared at 5:40 every evening. According to the locals, she was very punctual, too. She had chosen Medjugorje because she appreciated the fact that in 1933 a group of very strong people, men probably, had carried loads of cement to the top of Mount Križevac, built a cross there, and prayed for better crops. The Blessed Virgin first appeared on a hill near Mount Križevac that has since become known as Apparition Hill.

The news of the apparition spread quickly throughout Europe. Soon, tiny ugly Medjugorje was swarming with pilgrims. The government at the time felt threatened by the number of people visiting Medjugorje. They feared a "Candlelight Revolution." They banned all hikes to the top of Apparition Hill but no one took any notice. The pilgrims kept going to Medjugorje and climbing the hill, leaving behind a flag and a cross, and pinching a bit of dirt to take home as a souvenir. The expedition can take up to four hours.

I guess the Blessed Virgin decided to make things a little easier all round and started to appear to the visionaries in the sacristy of St. James Church. I'm sure they were quite happy with the change of venue for it sometimes reached minus 30 degrees on the hill. Standing there couldn't have been much fun, no matter what there was to look at.

I happened to be staying close to St. James Church in a guest house owned by Milka, the aunt of one of the visionaries. My company included four priests from Ireland, two nuns from Athens, and a few others.

"It's a pity you haven't been coming here more regularly," comments one of the priests.

Milka intervenes with excitement.

"President Bush one day sent limousine to collect my niece, Ivanka, to take her to Belgrade airport and then to the White House. He wanted to know what the Blessed Virgin was saying about Kuwait. He did not know what to do," she explains. "So Ivanka, she went to the White House to tell him."

On the main drag leading to St. James Church, the locals are congregating in groups of four and five. From what I can gather, they're planning the next day's climbing schedule so that not everyone is on top of the hill at once. Good idea! Someone has to be around to sell me coffee in case the dogma at the breakfast table gets too much and I have to make a quick exit.

"No problem," one of the pilgrims assures me. "That's why Mladen and his family climb each morning at three. They're always back in time to open their coffee shop."

The next thing I know, I'm approached by Mladen to join him and his family the following morning at three.

"No, thank you," I reply. "Maybe some other time."

Maybe not at all. Definitely not at three in the morning! Mladen was very understanding and thought it better, anyway, if I took the expedition with English-speaking pilgrims so that I could pray with them. Sure thing, Mladen.

Within twenty minutes of ending my conversation with him, I'm approached by four young people in their twenties: Jane, Sam, Phil and Mandy. They invite me to have breakfast with them the next morning. Somehow I knew

that a climb up the hill was also on the agenda and, of course, I was correct. We arrange to meet at seven. Not as bad as three, but bad enough. Jane, Sam, Phil and Mandy were in Medjugorje "for inspiration." Inspiration for what? I never found out. But talk about being the pigeon among cats!

The next morning my alarm clock goes off. I spring out of bed immediately. Can't afford a reputation of lacking in self discipline. Not in this place. I put on all the clothing I can find. I decide to throw myself in with an open mind. The truth is, I was seriously starting to question where in hell I was, and why.

I am the first to arrive at the coffee shop. Mladen is warming his hands on the cappuccino machine and greets me with way too much enthusiasm.

"My hands swelled so much from the cold that the stitching of my leather gloves broke," he tells me.

Oh God! Luckily the others arrived soon for I was seriously tempted to forget it and go back to bed, if not get out of Medjugorje altogether.

Jane, Sam, Phil and Mandy were full of love and happiness. I pretended that I was, too, but I wasn't really. Judging from the number of coats, scarves and gloves that we had on, I was certain that Apparition Hill would collapse the minute we ascended.

Too cold to talk, not yet awake enough to tell a joke or two, we start to trot toward the hill.

This certainly didn't have a going-for-a-picnic feel about it, that's for sure. No one spoke very much until we got to the foot of the hill. Then, Phil went on forever, praying to the Blessed Virgin that we would become less distracted by the cold so that our energy could become more focused on our love for God.

Sam, Phil, Mandy and Jane had ideas that they didn't initially reveal. I thought that we were going to climb to the top of the hill and back down again. Wrong! On the hill there are sixteen Stations of the Cross, beautiful bronze sculptures completed in 1987 by the Italian artist, Puzzolo. Taking turns, Sam, Phil, Mandy and Jane find lots to say at each of them. I find myself muttering the same thing over and over, "Please turn on the heat."

Phil had kindly bought me a prayer book so that I could join in with the group and pray for world peace. I prayed for the frostbite on my eyes, nose and ear lobes to disappear so that I could feel my face again. Whenever we opened our mouths to pray, our warm breath created

such a fog that from below it must have looked as if we were on fire. I wasn't meant to be observing the view from the top of the hill. I was meant to be looking up at the cross. I did for a bit, but after a while, a cross is a cross is a cross.

Climbing the hill took forever. Going down was no easier. A more difficult route was decided upon to test our tenacity. Dedication and suffering was the name of the game! The dedication was as impressive as the bronze sculptures, but the suffering was ridiculous.

At the bottom of the hill the rosary beads were selling like hot cakes. What a rip off! Thirty-two bucks! At first I thought they must have been the Blessed Virgin's personal set. But no, they were mass produced in Taiwan.

It didn't matter that the Vatican had not yet recognized Medjugorje in the way it had Fatima and Lourdes.

"She's here all right," says Phil.

Phil was from Queensland, Australia. He was completing a doctorate degree on the

reproduction habits of fruit flies in Northern New South Wales.

"I looked up at the clouds a few weeks ago and saw one shaped like the Blessed Virgin," he says. "I haven't been able to leave here since."

"I don't mean to be rude," I say, "but could it be that you're lonely or need some excitement in your life? I mean, spending years and years with fruit flies can't be much fun."

Clouds shaped like the Blessed Virgin! Give me a break. The locals said that in summer, Medjugorje was as busy as Disneyland. If Phil stayed in Medjugorje he was sure to get a job as Mickey Mouse.

Two days in Medjugorje was enough for me. Besides, the next day was Friday, and I wouldn't be allowed to eat or drink.

I went to the service at St. James Church at five o'clock. The church was so packed that I had to sit on the floor. At 5:40, apart from the footsteps of the visionaries who were ascending the stairs leading to the sacristy, there was total silence. Phil told me that a bell is rung when the Blessed Virgin has finished for the night. I did wonder if the bell he heard was in his head, but no, there it was, loud and clear. Tears flowed and everyone seemed to fall in love with everyone else.

The service soon came to a close. I was very eager to get back to Dubrovnik. Was that a bus I could hear? I quietly left the church. When I got outside, there was no bus, even though I was positive that I had heard one. Later, I was informed that a bus hadn't passed through Medjugorje since the morning.

Maybe I was hearing what I wanted to hear, in much the same way as I sometimes believe what I want to believe.

# Whadda'ya Gonna Do? Jump?

If you're into bondage and discipline, then you can't beat using public transport. You're expected to be well behaved on public transport. Some find this difficult despite warning notices threatening fines, imprisonment, castration or whipping by cane. Some may experience sudden urges ranging from fiddling with the volume switch of a boombox to exposing themselves. A pair of fluorescent sneakers may land on your seat. You may have to exercise self-control as the muddy sneaker, not content lying dormant, starts to wiggle toward your freshly dry-cleaned coat. You may feel like

knifing the foot in the sneaker, but chances are, if you're in New York City, a gun will be strapped to the ankle of that foot. In Rome, on a bus, you might get groped just to remind you of who's boss. You won't bother telling the driver. He might think that distraught women are cute and even cuter when ignored.

No one carries guns or commits sexual acts on Malta's buses. On Malta's buses everyone is fairly sedate, not because they're relaxed and enjoying the ride, but because they're praying for their safety! The drivers are so reckless that passengers have to grip firmly onto the backs of seats. Sometimes they say the Rosary together. This helps them ignore the bus driver's cursing. Don't worry if you don't have a set of rosary beads or if you don't know how to pray. Because of negligent and forgetful tourists like you the Maltese carry spare sets, and prayers are conveniently printed on the backs of seats.

Brightly painted golf balls act as handles on the ends of gear sticks. Sometimes, as a result of

Malta's bad roads and rotten drivers, the buses shake so much that these balls fall off and roll down the aisles and under seats. Drivers refuse to change gears without them. Passengers know that if they want to reach their set destination they had better poke their heads under their seats and find those golf balls. In the meantime the bus doesn't stop. The driver simply remains in whatever gear he's in, whether ascending a steep hill or rounding the sharp bend of an unmade road.

Neither can you be sure that once you get off the bus you'll be any safer than if you'd stayed on. Firstly, you're expected to jump off the minute the bus stops, so as not to waste any time. This means preparing in advance and standing behind the driver and the door. You do your best not to smash into the windscreen and you beg the driver not to take off before you have both feet solidly on the ground. Then you start praying (if you haven't been already) for the driver not to run you over as he takes off. These buses burn gallons of oil and leave clouds of soot behind. So, the final challenge is to be off the bus in one piece and not to end up looking like a panda.

Despite the rattling and rolling that passengers have to endure on Malta's buses, there's no better venue for instant relationships, whether you want them or not. These will vary in quality from a somewhat lonely character killing time, riding around Malta annoying the driver with endless chit chat, to an ex-crim seeking assistance from a total stranger.

"Excuse me," he says, "I hear you say that you are Australian. Is it all right if I talk to you? Maybe you can help me. You see, I am very sorry for what I did. I kill someone. Not really my fault. He make me very angry. Nobody blamed me, except his family, of course. I was put in jail for murder. And then, when I was in the jail, my wife and my children left me and went to live in England and now I can't find them. Do you mind if I speak to you in Maltese? I will be more comfortable."

He chats on while I drift away to those cold, frosty London mornings when I had to get up and go to work.

Like a reliable old dog, I'd walk to the Underground, forgiving it for any occurrence the night before. All you want is to get to work on time, but sometimes you don't. A train could break down, someone could inconsiderately throw himself onto the tracks, or leaves could accumulate under the wheels making it impossible for the train to travel uphill.

On the London Underground, familiarity with strangers is inevitable. Everyone always falls on top of everyone else. If you're seated, you also fall because the train tracks are very rough. It's simply not possible to maintain any level of decorum when you're flying around at a 360 degree angle and land on a stranger's lap.

"Excuse me. May I remain seated on your lap?"

No answer. This is a sophisticated banker who's about to get off at Liverpool Street. You take advantage of the situation and remain

seated on his lap. You may even be daring enough to put an arm around his shoulder for extra support. Sharing his newspaper is another option. He'd never swear in public. He may say "Pardon me!" a little assertively while wiggling uncomfortably. If he really gets irritated, he may say "Bollocks!" twice as loudly as his previous "Pardon me!"

The trains in London get so packed that passengers have to mold their bodies around the doors. You hold on tightly to your stuff because these are the circumstances that make a zipper easy to open and a wallet easy to snatch. You feel someone nudging you. You don't take much notice. After all, it's peak hour. Then you notice that the zipper of your bag is open and realize what's happened. There isn't much you can do. The thief has got off at the last stop and the train's now gaining speed.

In New York, body contact on a subway train, if it isn't sexual, usually spells theft, too. Hanging onto the hand rails above your head you hope that no one will decide to bend down and walk off with your shopping, which you've placed on the ground between your feet. If you yell, no one will take any notice, because in New York everyone's always yelling about something.

The Wall Street businessmen are yelling, competing with the punks from Brooklyn with their boomboxes and fluorescent sneakers.

When you ride the New York subways, human rights take on a whole new meaning. If you're the size of a Sumo wrestler you're allowed to take up as many seats as you need. Four youths get on at 125th Street in Harlem. They need everyone to vacate the aisles because they're about to perform some spectacular break dancing routine after which they'll pass around a hat. The homeless man sitting in the corner proves incontinent, and passengers have to bear the consequences. On New York subways, you have the right to be overweight, dance for your supper or pee in your pants if you want.

I need to get off at the next stop, and so I make my way toward the door. The train comes to a halt. A blind man stands at the platform. He pokes his stick around trying to find the carriage door. His stick gets stuck in the hem of my dress and finds its way to my navel.

"Hey buddy! Will you move your stick to some other place so the lady can get off the train," yells an irate passenger. "Because of you she's blocking the door, and I gotta get some place in a hurry."

"Just as well it's a stick he's got and not a dog," giggles someone in the background.

"I'll have a stick and a dog if I want. It's a free country!" the blind man retaliates.

You need to know which exit to take once you get off a train in New York. Some are used as urinals, some as bedrooms. You wouldn't want to invade anyone's privacy. Neither would you want to land your stiletto in a puddle of urine. You might get angry and scream and then someone might shoot you for making too much noise.

In New York, buses are usually less stressful than trains. Slower, yes. But less stressful. However, whether traveling by train or by bus, establishing eye contact with another commuter, whether by accident or not, guarantees conversation.

On a bus traveling to the Lower East Side, a woman sits with a bag of potato chips on her lap. She is determined to finish the lot by the time she gets off the bus. Just as many land on the floor as are being shoveled into her mouth. I keep my eyes focused on her because I think she's going to explode. She catches me looking at her and assumes that this is an invitation to tell me her life story.

"My doctor says I'm obese. That's why I got two dogs. I knew I'd have to walk 'em and that would be my exercise. But they didn't like walking and I didn't like picking up their poop, not even with my pooper scooper. Besides, I developed really bad in-grown eyelashes. Not just one, but a whole field of 'em. The doctor said it was from the stress of the dogs. I was doing real dumb stuff like sticking the Q-Tip too far into my ears so that the stick came out but the cotton didn't."

"Only the good Lord knows how much cotton's lodged in her head by now," comments an Irish woman who's sitting at the back of the bus.

"No one's talking to you asshole. You're not even from here. Why don't you go back to where you come from and grow more potatoes?"

"Why don't you stop eating 'em! You're going to blow up if you're not careful. Can't imagine anyone making love to you. He'd have to fight the flesh to find anything."

The bus stops. Some passengers get off. Others get on. The bus takes off again.

"Hey! Wait a minute. Stop. Stoppp!" the passengers yell in unison.

The bus suddenly halts and the driver yells, "What's wrong with all of you? I'm off schedule. You wanna see me fired?"

"A man's arm is locked in the door. You've taken off and he's still on the street. He didn't get on in time and you locked the door on him you jerk!"

The driver opens the door and a very angry man wearing a yarmulke gets on. The driver cuts him off before he has a chance to complain.

"I'm damned if I know how your arm could have been near the door when you were a block away. Just get on asshole. I'm off schedule. You're gonna get me fired," the driver repeats.

A woman wearing a crooked wig lifts her head from behind The New York Post and says, "Can we get a move on. I've gotta get to the hospital. My husband's in there. Can hardly recognize him anymore. Just had surgery. Walking around like a lunatic. You'd think the doctors and nurses would take better care of him. I mean, we pay our taxes, right? Walking around with his ass hanging out of his nightdress. Didn't even tie it up proper for him. Lucky I go see him regularly so I can tie it up for him. I mean I do the best I can. We all do. We all have to suffer."

"Oh God!" exclaims the woman with the potato chips. "Now we're gonna hear the whole damn story."

"So? You had your turn, didn't you, flesh feast?" objects the Irish woman.

The driver halts recklessly, reminding the

passengers, yet again, that he's off schedule. He isn't going to stop until there are at least three people waiting to get on or off the bus. No one dares argue because they know that if he's driving the same route the next day and recognizes them, he might not pick them up. You can't afford to upset a New York City bus driver.

In Tokyo, everything runs like clockwork. The Japanese spend more time on trains and subways than they do in bed. So, as you'd expect, trains are full of quiet, sleepy passengers.

An empty beer can rolling down the aisle would be fun. A fight would be even better. Wallet snatchers and gropers would be too much to ask for, and a smelly armpit is out of the question. Just as well, for under every passenger's armpit rests another passenger's head. The worst you'd expect would be for a bead of sweat to roll off someone's forehead and onto your handbag. But this wouldn't happen anyway because, for the Japanese, it's a cardinal sin not to carry a Christian Dior or

Yves St. Laurent towelette to wipe that sweaty brow. Should that towelette fall, it will never hit the ground. Packed? Crowded? Squashed like sardines? Suffice to say, when the doors fly open, people fly out, uncontrollably, as if they've just been released from a giant compressor and have only one minute to live.

In Tokyo, foreigners pray for something out of the ordinary to happen so as to kill the silence created by twelve million people who would rather stick needles in their eyes than cause a disturbance. I guess my prayers were answered.

One afternoon I find myself on an express train traveling from Yokohama to Tokyo. Five teenagers with hair dyed all colors of the rainbow decide to sit on the floor near the door. They are admiring each other's jewelry, which consists of safety pins inserted into ears and nostrils or made into necklaces and anklets. One of them takes two safety pins from her jacket lapel and adds these to the ones in her ear lobes, thus creating a dangling effect. The teenagers are loud and raucous and proud of their rebellious behavior.

The Ginza set and the salarymen look around disapprovingly. The Japan Railway employee doesn't know what to do, so he stands in the corner of the carriage with his hands behind his back. Clad in a spotless navy blue uniform, white gloves, and a cap secured by a chin strap, he anxiously waits for the train to stop and hopes that the teenagers will get off. But they don't. When the train door opens, a butterfly finds its way into the carriage, at which point the teenagers cover their heads and start screaming. This is most un-Japanese and has to stop immediately, especially as there are a couple of foreigners on the train, including myself.

The poor JR employee runs off into another carriage and soon returns with a pale green insect swat. While the teenagers continue screaming and embarrassed passengers start to look for needles to poke into their eyes, the JR employee runs up and down the carriage

trying to swat the butterfly. Finally he corners it, but to his dismay, a youth wearing an "Animal Rights" badge, aggressively snatches the insect swat from his hand and begins abusing him.

The Ginza set with their designer shopping bags soon get off the train in disgust, and with them the butterfly escapes freely. The animal rights activist looks around proudly. He truly has a success story to tell at his next group meeting.

The salarymen are still asleep. The JR employee wipes the sweat from his brow that was caused by the most embarrassing moment in his career. He begins to worry that perhaps he didn't handle the butterfly incident the way the boss would have wanted and has now lost all possibility of promotion. He wishes the punks would get off the train and free the passengers and him from their presence, but the punks are quite happy sitting on the floor playing with their safety pins.

In Malta, the bus drivers are swearing because their golf balls won't attach securely to the ends of their gear sticks. They decide to go on strike there and then, "Until the government fixes the roads!" Passengers suddenly become hostages because, out of spite, drivers refuse to open the doors.

On at least one subway somewhere in New York someone is being mugged and has to accept it. Someone in Rome is being groped

Sinclair

and has to act as if she likes it. And in London, passengers are cursing under their breath because it's freezing and trains have been stationary for two hours. Leaves under wheels again! Everyone wants to get off but can't. Some hold onto window panes and out of frustration try to shake them open as prisoners sometimes do when locked in a cell.

# Moths, Braids and Shrimp Shells

Before entering Tasty, a cafe on the main drag of Chania, Crete, I resigned myself to the fact that by the time I left I would smell like an ashtray and my skin would need steam cleaning. My hair, about three feet long, would probably need a wash as well, which is normally okay, except on Crete, in winter, in a cheap hotel where hair dryers are prohibited because they use too much electricity.

"Look, you might choke from the cigarette smoke," said Vin.

"And the squat toilet might be blocked," added Viv.

"But you'll have a beaut experience," they declared in unison.

Vin and Viv were two young Australians from Norfolk Island, traveling around the world looking for "beaut" experiences and trying to have a baby. Their latest adventure before coming to Crete was living on top of Mount Sinai with the Bedouins. Apparently, the Bedouins didn't like doing much except sitting in tents all day smoking, drinking, eating, and occasionally getting up and about whenever the need for copulation arose. Vin thought that the area the Bedouins used as a toilet could do with a bit of tiling and so got free lodging for a month in exchange for laying a few tiles, a ten-minute job. Needless to say, it wasn't the sort of accommodation that was conducive to baby making.

Thanks to Vin, the Bedouins now think that Aussies are the hardest workers in the world and are therefore always welcome on top of Mount Sinai. Vin and Viv promised never to tell the Commonwealth Employment

Service back home in Australia in case they came up with some weird and wonderful scheme for the unemployed that included a trip to Mount Sinai.

Inside, Tasty was not only smoky, but slippery as well. You couldn't see, nor could you walk without risking a nose dive.

The owner sees us coming. Realizing that he isn't making any money from his friends who've been sitting for at least an hour without ordering food or drink, he orders them to vacate their table for us. Tourists were scarce, not only because of the bad weather, but also because of the proximity of Crete to the Persian Gulf, where a war was in full swing at the time.

We sit down, and the first thing I do is rest my elbow in a puddle of oil. The plastic table-cloths are covered with at least an inch of oil, fat and grease. Vin starts carving "I love Viv" into the grease, proud that he isn't actually scratching the plastic. The lime and orange ashtrays have also suffered a few melting moments at the hands of clumsy cigarette smokers.

Through the smog I see an elegant Cretan staring directly at me. He looks great, dressed in tight black fisherman's pants tucked into hand-made knee high boots. A beautiful hand-knitted woolen sweater accompanies all this and, to set everything off, he wears a black crocheted cap with dangling beads. The Cretan version of an Aussie cork hat. A real live Zorba! Our eyes meet, mine admiringly, I have to admit. He proceeds to join our table, and because we don't shoo him away, a few others, including three Arabs wearing anti-Saddam Hussein T-shirts, assume that they can join our table as well. They must have been freezing, but probably thought it was better to be freezing on Crete than dying in Kuwait.

So there I was in a typical Greek cafe in Chania, Crete. On my right was Zorba, who had since introduced himself as the "King of Crete." Another, calling himself the "German Animal," was on my left. I was in the middle, subject to the spillage from clinking glasses, and to flying shrimp shells, which the King spat out with great gusto. I quickly buttoned up my shirt so that I didn't end up with shrimp shells in my cleavage. Choke, cough, splutter, dodge a shrimp shell and welcome to Crete. As the German Animal starts to play with my hair, the King picks up my hand and starts to read my palm.

"Your life is going to be short," he announces.

"It can't be," I reply. "I've got too much to do."

"Forget it. You won't be able."

His next comment is just as profound.

"You look like a woman, but inside of you, you're not. You haven't got the feeling. Your feeling is that of a man."

All this might sound funny, and retro-spectively it is, but at the time the King was upsetting me greatly. Not because of his flying shrimp shells. But because some of this geezer's kitchen wisdom was hitting home, by accident of course, but hitting home all the same. Not the stuff about being more like a bloke than a woman. I suspect that was in expectation of me saying, "Okay. Come to bed and I'll show you I'm all woman" or some other Mae Westish type of line. But his comment that my life would be short was disconcerting. I mean, Iraq had just bombed Israel, and Suda Bay, where there was a United States military base, was just down the road from my hotel. The Cretans were getting nervous, and so was I. There hadn't been as much activity in Suda Bay since World War II. One couldn't see the water for warships. The cafes were full of American soldiers nervously munching on Cretan style hamburgers, not quite what they were used to.

"What star sign are you?" asks the King. "I studied astrology in Canada. I can tell everything about you."

"Libra. Tell me something nice," I plead.

"Nothing to say," he replies, as he spits out a shrimp's kneecap.

In the meantime, the German Animal on my left had created a braid with my hair. However, it wasn't made pretty by cute dried pink and white flowers. Instead, it was adorned with shrimp shells, for the King insisted on spitting these out and aiming them at me. I was glad that the King had only one shrimp left on his plate. I wondered where it would land. I was starting to look like a beachfront.

Speaking of beachfronts, if you were to take a walk along the beachfront of Chania between six and eight in the morning, you would see a fellow nicknamed Peter the Submarine. You'd

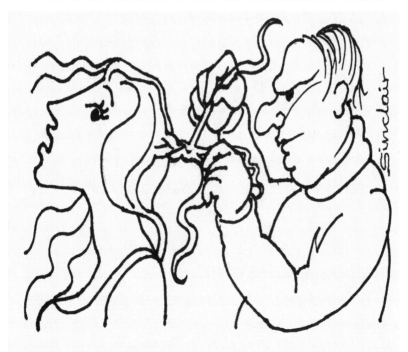

know it was him because he'd be the only one stupid enough to be in the water when it was still thawing. He would dive in and pretend to be a submarine. Peter was about thirty years old and from Switzerland. He complained that Switzerland was too conservative. He was interested in warfare, and as Switzerland wasn't particularly promoting it, he'd decided on Crete. Why Crete? No one ever found out, but everyone told him that he'd got off at the wrong stop. It was the Middle East he wanted. Anyway, when Peter wasn't in the water playing submarines, he'd be marching through the streets of Chania in full army gear as if he'd just come out of the jungle. Every now and then he pretended he was throwing a hand-grenade. Of course, the King and the German Animal were his best friends, although there wasn't a common language among them.

When Peter the Submarine walked into Tasty, everyone fell silent.

"Watch this! Watch this!" whisper Vin and Viv.

Peter shuts the door of the restaurant and marches to our table. He is guarding an imaginary rifle. The King and the German Animal slowly rise and begin making guttural sounds, which gradually reach a crescendo. Peter joins them halfway. Their arms meet over my head and somehow, the heaviest of the three, the German Animal, lands on top of Peter's head.

"They're pretending they're orangutans. It happens every time they meet," Viv whispers.

At Tasty the night started to drag. I was beginning to think that I was in Crete's loony bin.

Suddenly the King turns to me and says, "You're frightened of madness, eh? You're mad."

Believe me, the initial effect of the great-looking Zorba with the dangling beads was wearing off quick smart.

"I went mad a long time ago and have never been happier," exclaims the King. "My wife went mad too. She went mad before me, but that was a different kind of madness. Her madness was because of an insect."

Viv and Vin look at each other. Could the King possibly be screwing up his vocabulary?

"An insect?" I ask.

"Yes. A moth!" he replies.

On hearing the word "moth," Peter and the German Animal jump on top of the table and start flapping their arms and making buzzing sounds. They laugh loudly, for they obviously know the story well. The King gestures for them to sit down and shut up as their Retsina was spilling all over the place. He obviously hadn't told them that it's bees that buzz, and not moths.

"Plenty of moths on Crete in summer. One went straight into her ear. It was ... how you say ... fluttering, and then got stuck there in the wax. It died, but she felt it flutter for years until she went mad. Pretty funny, eh? I'm glad she experienced some fluttering before she died. There was no flutter from me. I didn't like her, not even when we got married."

Viv and Vin are laughing their heads off, and soon so is everyone else. With the laughter, the Arabs see an opportunity to start clapping rhythmically. Within a few minutes, tables and chairs are thrown out of the way and Tasty becomes a Cretan reggae room. Peter and the German Animal, however, decide to dance the waltz.

I didn't care about the Retsina spilling all over me, but I did start to worry when the German Animal attempted to lodge me between his knees as if I were his horse, using the braid he had created earlier as a rein. Viv and Vin give me a look that reminds me of their promise when we first entered Tasty. We were certainly having an experience, although "beaut" was not how I would've described it.

"I want to go now Vin," says Viv. "I'm going to try and get up early tomorrow and get a job for the day."

If you want to make an extra quid while on Crete, you go to the main square in the center of Chania at seven in the morning and line up with everyone else for a day of olive or orange picking and occasionally other jobs as well. You don't have a say as to whether you get to pick olives or oranges, and if you're female, you often don't get selected to work at all, in which case you go back home to bed. Olive picking entails beating a tree with full force and then searching the ground for the olives. You have to look tough and willing to beat trees. I didn't look like the tree beating type, so I didn't get ushered into the truck for olive pickers. Unlike

Viv, I wasn't tall, so I didn't get selected for orange picking. I wasn't left behind, though. Oh, no no no. Two other short, passive-looking American gals and I were ushered into a four-wheel drive to do "a very special job," one especially for women, we were told.

The driver took no notice of the fact that none of us could speak Greek. He just kept yakking in Greek while we yakked among ourselves in English. Naturally, we were curious as to how we would be spending the day.

Annie felt certain that his wife had just left him and we were going to have to cook a month's worth of meals. Deanna thought we would be washing a month's worth of socks and jocks. All I was worried about was that he might have wanted a month's worth of our bodies, singularly, or all at once. Finally, after our guesswork was exhausted, we arrived at his farmhouse.

"Thank God," we utter in unison, as we see a washing line full of clothes.

Soon we see about six hundred identical

dogs, and then comes our boss's wife, who looks like a shepherdess, and could have been, except that it was dogs she was tending and not sheep. Jorgo, our boss, takes us to a shed, and for eight hours, less fifteen minutes for lunch, the three of us clean up dog shit. And all for twenty bucks each! Needless to say, no one ate during lunch break.

"Twenty bucks is better than nothing," says Jeff, another of the gorgeous hippie remnants living on Crete to escape repression, suppression, depression, marriage or maintenance. "It'll buy you two nights' accommodation and four souvlakis at Tasty," he teases.

I'd just finished telling Jeff about my exciting day and the experience at Tasty the night before.

"You'll find it hard to leave Chania even if you're not having a good time. I've been here for nine years and hardly ever have a good time, but I'm still here," he says earnestly.

I didn't know whether to laugh or cry. He was actually talking about the "mind space" people get into when they live in Chania. Chania made you sit back, relax, say yes to everything and develop the patience of a saint. Sudden storms threatening to drag you out to sea, wine glass and all, the same order of food arriving at your table for the second time, unreliable bus and ferry timetables, but most of all, what the locals had to say about life; all this you had to take as it came, or like some, you'd go mad.

Some people travel in order to find the meaning of life, and they don't go home until they find it. Jeff kept thinking that he'd found it, but then, just as he was about to go home, he changed his mind and stayed on Crete to look further. In fact, Jeff and his quest to find the meaning of life had become a standing joke on Crete. Poor Jeff. He was greeted with, "Found it yet, Jeff?" or, "Hey, Jeff, you just walked past it."

Chances are that characters like Jeff, the German Animal, Peter the Submarine, the King, and all the other lunatics I met on Crete, have exhausted the locals and are looking for someone new with whom to share their madness. Tourists are great bait. Locals can smell tourists a mile away, and it isn't just because they're carrying backpacks and maps either.

It will take years of therapy before I can ever feel comfortable around moths. I'll burn my hair before I allow anyone to braid it again, and shrimp is now definitely off the menu.

# My My Malta

Everyone in my family was born in Malta, except for my brother and me. Malta is a small island smack bang in the middle of the Mediterranean. At family gatherings my parents and relatives entertained themselves with stories from the *old* world. Some heart wrenching, some hilarious. Most of them exaggerated, I'm sure. The stories always included eccentric characters with nicknames that didn't make sense when translated into English. These misfits upset the status quo with their presence and their differences. Where they came from, what they were doing in Malta, and where they ended up, provided material for hours of discussion around the kitchen table in my parents' house in Melbourne, Australia. Details of the stories were as different as day and night, depending on who was telling them and how loud the storyteller was.

Friends have always bugged me to go to Malta in search of my roots. People admit to having *found* themselves this way. Me? I never had any such desire. I've always found enough about myself in need of fixing without going out and looking for more. Nevertheless, I thought that I should at least see the place sometime or other before I die. I was in Naples and there was a ferry going to Malta, and so I jumped on. I knew only too well that I would spend most of the journey with my head hanging over the edge being sick. When it comes to motion sickness, I'm the world's worst, and, after this trip, I was sure to make it into the Guinness Book of Records.

This ferry was very basic. There were garbage bins, rows of fold-up tin chairs,

bathrooms, a tea and coffee machine, and a cold water tap with a column of paper cups. You knew to keep your cup for later since there were a lot more passengers than there were paper cups. This ferry was nothing like those luxury ones you see in those advertisements that keep popping up on your computer screen or like the ones plastered all over the walls and windows of travel agencies.

I grab a chair and hope for the best, but, as expected, I'm sick as a dog the minute the ferry starts sailing. By the time we reached Malta, I wasn't sure if the ferry had flipped over or whether my stomach had turned inside out. Sitting close to me are two men saying the Rosary together, in Maltese. I lift my head for a moment, giving them the opportunity to introduce themselves. They are Mario Camilleri and Mario Camilleri. Malta has a population of a little over 400,000 and, as one would expect, there isn't a great variety of last names.

"Are you all right?" asks one of the Marios. "The sea is very rough. Is it all right if we talk to you? Maybe it will help to take your mind from being sick. We like very much to talk to tourists. You can talk to them about everything."

"Your suitcase, it looks very heavy," comments the other Mario, "but you look like you've got very strong hands. Good for massaging my back. I have a very sore back from picking up all the fruits thrown onto the ground at the market. You massage my back, I give you my fruit. What is your name?"

Guessing that they mean no harm, I laugh at their forwardness and introduce myself. Pulo is also a Maltese last name, though not a common one because most of the Pulos have died off.

They talk lovingly about their children and grandchildren and ask if I have any. I shake my head. They complain about their wives and ask if I'm married. I shake my head. They stare at each other for a moment wondering what might be wrong with me. They ask what I do for a living. I say I'm an actress. Out come the rosary beads again. I ask them to pray that I make it to

Malta with my organs intact and not to worry too much about the marriage and no-babies stuff, or my job. They assure me that they can pray for more than one thing at a time. I pray that they get their priorities right.

I ask them if they can recommend a cheap place for me to stay while in Malta. I'd been traveling for several months and I was broke.

"There's a very cheap place in Buggieba. It's called Manny's Place. The landlord, his name is Manny. He is a very good man. Quite a gentleman. We have known him for long time. But he is not very ... sophisticated. He went a little, how you say? Funny ... in the head. After his mother died. First his mother, then his father. He has two dogs. They were a present when he retired from his job. Him and his dogs stay in one room, and anyone who want, they pay him something and they stay in the other rooms."

Cheap with a funny-in-the-head, dog-loving landlord named Manny (same name as my funny-in-the-head uncle in Australia). Good

enough for me.

After twenty-five hours we arrive in Malta and disembark at Valletta Harbour. As the ferry gates open I see that the harbor is truly magnificent, just as my family promised. I can't understand it, but my eyes fill with tears. Maybe it's those roots that everyone keeps telling me to go and find.

The two Marios are greeted by their wives and they introduce me to them. Their names are Mary Camilleri and Mary Camilleri. They look at me suspiciously, wondering what their ripe and ready husbands did to amuse themselves on the long boat trip from Naples. The two Marios quickly announce that my family is from Malta and now lives in Australia. Suddenly I'm okay to the two Marys, who start hugging and kissing me and pinching my cheeks as if I'm a long lost relative who's finally found her way home. They offer any assistance I may need while in Malta because anyone with Maltese blood in their veins is family. That's all there is to it. They don't give me their addresses or telephone numbers. There's no need. If I'm in Malta for more than a week, I'm sure to bump into them and can be certain that they'll remember me, ask how I am and give me the food from their mouths if I'm hungry.

It's mid afternoon on Thursday. The sun is warm and welcoming. Everything looks so old, so mysterious and so incredibly beautiful. I feel like I'm stepping back into my family's childhood. And, for the second time, my eyes fill with tears. Something tells me that I'd better get used to this.

To get to Manny's Place in Buggieba I have to catch a bus from the central bus terminal in Valletta, Malta's capital. Valletta is known as the Mediterranean center for steeples, steps and bells. There are many churches, all Roman Catholic. I see women sweeping sidewalks, cleaning windows, polishing doors and balconies, and hanging out washing. I see the Mediterranean, which is within walking distance. I smell the salt, carried by the breeze from the ocean. I take deep breaths. I feel so healthy and energetic despite what I had to endure to get here.

There are many Maltese pastry stalls at the bus terminal, and I am starving. After all, there's nothing left in my stomach. I buy a couple of *pastizzi*, a traditional Maltese snack food: diamond-shaped pastry filled with either ricotta or a spicy pea mixture. My mother and aunt in Australia make these (and just as good), but there's something special about eating them here. As I'm eating my *pastizzi* and waiting for the bus to Buggieba, I'm approached by a fishmonger named Joey, who asks if I have room in my suitcase for a *lampuka*.

"What's a *lampuka*?" I ask in Maltese.

"Fresh Mediterranean fish," he replies in English.

He hands me a frozen one, wrapped and ready to go.

"I'm the only fisherman who sells fresh *lampuki* in Valletta. Valletta is my territory," he says proudly.

The atmosphere is peaceful and relaxing. No one treads on anyone else's toes. You have to ask Joey if it's okay with him to sell fresh *lampuki* in Valletta. If it isn't, tough luck. You have to find somewhere else to sell your fish.

With a *lampuka* in my suitcase, I board the bus to Buggieba, hoping not to be sold a rabbit or a pigeon along the way. All three are traditional Maltese dishes.

Approximately half an hour later the driver yells, "Buggieba. Everybody get off!" I find my way to Manny's Place. The door is ajar. I enter, and the first thing I see, proudly exhibited in the reception area, is a beautifully polished trophy awarded to Manny by the Floriana Fire Station. Everything else in the place appears to be falling apart. The arms and legs of the wicker chairs are scratched and splintered and look as if they've been nibbled at by the dogs the two Marios had mentioned, and the cushions are

gradually becoming disemboweled. The marble floor is discolored, and weeds are growing between the cracks. The lace curtains are frayed and unevenly hung. On the window ledges, coffee table and television, are dusty, chipped porcelain statuettes of Dalmatian dogs. All of them cute. Sleeping. Eating. Running. Jumping. Pooping. One is lying on a recliner wearing sunglasses and an "I Love Malta" T-shirt.

Soon I meet the real thing: Manny's two Dalmatian dogs. They stroll casually downstairs, circle my suitcase, sniff the fish and lick their lips. Just as casually, they return upstairs and reappear with someone whom I assume is Manny, their master. Manny introduces himself and his *family*, Donald and Dolores. (Thank God their names aren't Mario and Mary.) He pats and hugs them. They return his affections with big sloppy licks to the front and back of his overalls.

Manny appeared kind-hearted, but it was difficult to take him seriously for he did all he could to resemble his dogs. He had a full head of gray hair that was splashed with black dye, and he wore black and white polka-dotted overalls.

"Don't worry about the dogs," says Manny. "They're very quiet. They only bark when I bark. And don't be scared if you hear a noise in the night like scratching on the wall. They like to eat the plaster. Welcome to Malta."

I took an immediate liking to Manny, and he soon proved to be the gentleman that he was reputed to be, and equally as eccentric.

It's no wonder that Manny's Place never made its way into any of the travel guides. A five star hotel would definitely have been more comfortable, but nowhere could have been more entertaining. And nothing could ever have prepared me for the nuts that I met there.

When sharing a room with strangers, you pray for no snorers, farters, sleepwalkers or talkers. Well, I happened to be with four others who did the whole lot at once as if synchronized. I wondered if John Cage had set this up and was hiding somewhere with a microphone. It seemed that every eccentric on a budget who comes to Malta comes to Manny's Place.

There was Elsie, who occupied the bunk above me. Whenever I lifted my head, I hit her in the butt. The mattresses weren't very firm and drooped onto your face if the person in the bunk above was heavy-set. Elsie wasn't only heavy-set but snored as she breathed in and passed wind when she breathed out.

Lana slept on an armchair in the corner under four fully opened black umbrellas. (I'm sure she slept better than anybody else, too.) She was obsessed with changing their design. If she had come to Malta for inspiration, she had definitely come to the wrong place. Malta enjoys a great deal of sunshine, and it rains very little in the daytime.

Philippe and Takayuki shared the double bunk on the other side of the room and had become good friends. Philippe had tried to make a living from playing the violin outside various music venues in Europe. His knowledge of music venues was genuine. His violin playing was not. He carried a boombox and a collection of Stéphane Grappelli CDs. He had learned to mimic the Austrian violinist very well. A good trick, he thought, until someone discovered that he was a fraud.

Takayuki spent most of his time walking around Malta taking photographs. One day he set off for St. Paul's Catacombs in Rabat, near the medieval town of Mdina. He had so much photographic equipment on his back that he looked like Mount Fuji on the move. At the catacombs, Takayuki thought he saw a ghost and dropped his camera.

That night I was kept awake not only by

Elsie's snoring and farting, and Donald and Dolores chewing at the walls, but by Takayuki crying over his ruined camera and Philippe trying to pacify him, to no avail. Then, when I finally did doze off, I was awakened by Lana, who let out a scream. One of the umbrellas had collapsed on top of her. She is now convinced that umbrellas are out to get her because she's trying to change their image. I needed to get out of this place.

In the morning I decide to skip breakfast and the madness and mayhem at Manny's Place and to go and take some photographs. Before leaving Naples, I had received a phone call from my mother.

"Hurry up and send us some photographs. I was born at 97 St. Nicholas Street and baptized at St. Dominic's. Both are in Valletta. When I was five we moved to Gzira and lived at 45 Stuart Street. Gzira is full of prostitutes now, but don't worry about them, go anyway. I went to the green government school. Your father went to St. Aloysius in Birkirkara. But he hated it there. So if you run out of time, just forget that one. But don't forget your grandfather's tailor shop. He was there from 1895 to 1931."

I set off with my camera and am surprised at how emotional I feel. There really is something moving about being in the places where my parents and ancestors were born, bred and educated. I can't help thinking that if grandpa hadn't taken the whole clan to Australia, this is where I would've been born, too.

A photograph of my father playing soccer, dated 1932, is hanging on a wall in the corridors of St. Aloysius. 45 Stuart Street, Gzira, now houses Gzira's football club. St. Dominic's is still there. Churches always are. The green government school is now pink. Grandpa's old tailor shop is still a tailor shop and his sewing machine is still sitting in the window. I don't know exactly how I'm going to tell my mother that the house in which she was born now belongs to Roberta and Francine, two Maltese transvestites.

I catch a bus to the Addolorata, Malta's largest cemetery, in the suburb of Marsa. I want to find my grandparents' graves. I walk around in a daze, for hours it seems. On each of the tombstones I see photographs of people who don't look like strangers: people who look like my parents' friends and people who look like our neighbors in St. Albans, a suburb of Melbourne where there is a large Maltese population and where I lived until my late teens. Suddenly, I see *my* face in a photograph on a tombstone! It's my Aunt Mary. My father always said I looked like his sister. I guess it's true.

On the way back from the cemetery, I detour through Paceville, where most of Malta's nightlife is found. I see a notice on the door of AXIS, a discotheque, advertising for a bathroom attendant. Three nights a week from 4 p.m. to 4 a.m. Perfect! I wasn't getting much sleep during these hours at Manny's Place anyway.

At AXIS I meet three hundred women, three times a night, each with the same recipes for *lampuki*, rabbit, pigeon and life. One by one, they enter, shake their magnificent heads of spiral permed hair, check their tummies and bottoms from all angles, and then say, "I have to go on a diet." As one leaves another enters, and the exercise is repeated. Oh, what fun it is when there are a few there at the same time exercising in unison. Their timing is impeccable, for this dance is not only well choreographed, but very well rehearsed.

One woman, Carmen, isn't as preoccupied with dancing as some of the other women and prefers to sit in the bathroom and talk to me. She is studying pharmacology.

"It's not a waste of time for me to study," she says. "After I graduate I can work until I have children. And I still have to get married. I will be able to use my education for at least another two years. In that time I will make enough money to buy the furniture. He will buy the house."

"Oh, you have a boyfriend then?" I ask.

"No, but it won't be difficult when the time comes. Here in Malta we all want the same thing. So one man or woman is as good as the other."

Carmen asks me about my travels and what it's like to live abroad. She is bewildered to hear that I feel comfortable traveling alone.

"But where do you want to settle down?" she asks.

"New York," I respond, without wasting a second. "It'd be like a dream come true. But first I have to get a green card and they're not easy to get."

"But your family is not in New York, and New York is very dangerous. Why do you want to live there?" she asks.

"It's exciting and I feel so at home there. I love New York," I say.

"I love Malta," she responds, also without wasting a second. "Too much excitement is not good for you. Malta's not very exciting, but we don't have many problems. We only have one prison, in Paola, and there are only a few people in it. Most of them are foreigners."

In Malta the people are like my Maltese family in Australia: generous, helpful, warm and friendly. But, although Malta is where my blood comes from, I didn't feel like I had *come home* in any way. I had arrived in Malta on a boat that rocked all the way from Naples, but, as I quickly learned, there was no rocking the boat once I got there.

Independence, ambition, having a mind of one's own and the courage to be defiant and forthright, qualities that I value and nurture in myself, aren't qualities that are encouraged in women, or men, in small, peaceful and religious Malta.

For the Marios, Marys and Carmens, living in Malta is truly fine. For me, Malta was an exercise in tolerance and compassion, a series of lonely moments and revelations, and finally, an understanding and acceptance of my family and my roots and some of the things that make me, me.

# In the Land of the Pooper Scoopers

**W**henever I tell anyone about the saga of getting a green card and moving to New York, everyone says the same thing: "Why didn't you just find some American guy, give him some money and get him to marry you like in that movie *Green Card*?" (Australian director, by the way.) "It would've been cheaper." Cheaper? Definitely! But simpler? I don't think so.

There were all these stories about how spies from the U.S. Immigration and Naturalization Service would break into your apartment to check if you both shared the same underwear

drawer. Or they'd call you in, without prior notice, and interview you separately and ask you if he had any "distinguishing marks such as tattoos or piercings on his private parts." And, of course, if you weren't really married, or at least in a relationship, you wouldn't know.

I didn't marry anyone for my green card. I missed out three times in the green card lottery, when Australia was finally one of the countries included in the lottery. Didn't buy a green card, even though a shoemaker on the Lower East Side offered me one. Didn't do anything illegal. Didn't pretend I was a student, a model or a nanny. Neither did I pretend I was a nun so that I could get a religious visa. (I learned that those exist, too.) On May 22, 1993, I was the first Australian to be made a lifetime member of The Actors Studio, and after much sweat, tears and money, I got an EB1 green card (Alien of Extraordinary Ability).

After the I.N.S. approved my petition, I had to attend an interview at the U.S. Consulate. I'm from Melbourne. The U.S. Consulate I had to go to is in Sydney, which is approximately 550 miles from Melbourne.

I sit in my hotel room at the Koala Travel Lodge on Oxford Street, Sydney, triple-checking that I have everything: current passport, two passport-size color photographs (three-quarter angle and no earrings), birth certificate, health clearance, police clearances from all the countries I've lived in for six months or longer (easy enough to get, except when one of the countries is Japan!), bank statements, letter of intent. Somewhere to live. Somewhere to work. Somewhere to die. Blood! They wanted blood! And they wanted even *more* money.

"Where's the health clearance?" asks the office assistant in a sugary sweet voice.

"What? It's there! It's there! I checked everything a thousand times."

"Oh! Here it is. Naughty. Hiding behind the big fat clip."

"Phew! You nearly gave me a heart attack. No! No! I didn't mean that. My heart's in really good nick. I promise. Well, health-wise, anyway."

"The Consul General will be with you shortly."

Please God. Make him greet me with a big friendly smile. He greets me.

"Miss Pulo. Your EB1 Visa has been approved and all your documents are in good order. Congratulations. In two weeks you'll receive a package. Carry it with you in your hand luggage. Don't lose it. Don't forget it at home. And whatever you do, don't open it! Have a safe trip, Miss Pulo."

Oh my God! This package. What's in it? You're not supposed to carry anything on an airplane if you haven't packed it yourself.

I arrive at J.F.K. with the package held tightly against my chest: my EB1 testimonials, as it turns out. Oh my God! I've forgotten my chest X-rays in my father's closet back home in Melbourne and I'm supposed to carry them in hand luggage too.

Luckily I'd packed a tin of Australian hard

candy, silly little kangaroos, koalas and kookaburras, which I'd bought at Melbourne Airport. I frantically pull out the tin of candy, open it, and offer the candy to the immigration officer hoping to distract him so that he doesn't ask for the X-rays, and it works.

He painstakingly examines each piece of candy and then says, "Next time don't forget ..."

My heart feels like it has stopped.

"... the shrimp on the barbie," he says menacingly. "May I see your passport, M'am?"

"Sure. Can't keep it though," I chuckle excitedly.

"I don't want to keep it, M'am. Just want to stamp it. See M'am, stamping passports is my job and I gotta do my job. That's a mighty good photograph of you, M'am, but it don't look like you. Are you sick today or just tired or something? I've been sitting here for thirty-three years. Don't know if I'm sick, tired or dead. Had a wife and six kids to feed. Now I've only got the wife. Food bill's the same though. Hey, you wanna take her back to Oustraylia with you? She's always saying she's gonna leave me. I'd like to try and make it a little easy for her. So, you've come to live in the good ole U S of A."

I knew of a comedian in Australia who could speak for hours without moving his face. This guy could do it, too, except he wasn't making anyone laugh.

"New York! I've come to live and work in New York. It's like a dream come true."

"A dream come true, ha? Just watch you don't get drugged, mugged, catch some weird disease or get thrown down the subway tracks. Those trains move pretty fast, M'am. Before you know it, you're hamburger meat. I'm not kidding. Happens every day. You can read about it in The New York Times, New York Post, Daily News, Newsday. Any place you want. Gotta be tough in the Big Apple. Don't let anyone mess with you. You know what I'm saying? Welcome to the United States of America, M'am."

I get out of the airport and into a cab.

"New York very expensive, Miss. Everything expensive. Ever have to bury your mother in New York? I tell you that was expensive. Not like where I come from. Everything cheap. Clothes cheap. Food cheap. Funeral cheap. Don't know why she just die like that. In New York! No warning. Nothing. Nada."

The cab driver then proceeded to complain about everything, from the cost of an apple to the cost of an orchard, all the way to Midtown Manhattan.

I get to the building I'm staying at, throw my suitcases into the apartment, and catch the elevator on its way back down. It's packed.

A woman enters. She has a dog, an enormous dog with that look of ecstasy on its face that all New York dogs have when they're descending a skyscraper and going for a walky poo.

"I suppose you're wondering where my pooper scooper is. With a dog this big I'd need a wheelbarrow. Much easier to keep it constipated."

I start to laugh.

"Don't laugh! My dog may be big, but it's sensitive, and strangers are expected to know that. Where do you come from anyway?"

"Australia."

"Oh! That figures. That's why you don't

know about dogs. You guys got them hopping things. Well, this is New York and New York's got dogs. Lots of them. You have to like dogs if you're gonna live in New York or you just gotta go back to where you come from."

I keep a straight face till I leave the building and then laugh all the way to the pretzel stand on the corner of 42nd Street and Eighth Avenue.

On the way there I meet a street vendor specializing in vintage comic books and posters. He introduces himself as Bob. His knees and elbows are heavily bandaged, not because of any injury, but in case a car happens to swerve onto the sidewalk where he's standing and knocks him over.

"See, when a car hits you from behind you usually fall on your knees first and then onto your elbows. I know. I've got hit a few times on the job. I'd be standing here minding my own business when wham! Some asshole who shouldn't be driving. Then there's all the street noise! I've tried everything to block it out.

Self hypnosis. Ear plugs. Even let my ears get blocked with the soot from the street. My girlfriend didn't like me doing that. Not that she ever gets close enough to me these days for it to matter. You know what I'm saying? We got problems. She's too critical. Hey, I got good stuff," he tells me proudly, changing the subject. "That's why I have to keep an eye on all the scumbags that come 'round here. And New York's full of scumbags, let me tell you. No one does their job properly anymore. Like yesterday. They call me up and tell me I have to go identify someone at the morgue. My father disappeared some time ago."

"Oh! I'm so sorry Bob," I say sympathetically.

"Well, we still don't know if he's dead or not. We alerted the authorities. So far not a trace. But every time some unidentified son of a bitch lands at the morgue they ask me to go in and identify the body. I visit the morgue these days more often than l go take a pee. But yesterday they really goofed. Dig this. They wheel out a guy that don't look nothing like my father. Not even close. This was a huge son of a bitch with a nose the size of my fist. My father was a small guy like me and had bad circulation in his feet. Lost a few of his toes. Then they had to amputate his foot. This guy they wheel out has two feet and ten toes. I counted 'em. So this confirmed it straight away. I mean, you don't grow your foot back once it's cut off, do you? Anyway, whenever you don't see me here you know where l am. At the morgue. Except from now on I'm going to ask if the body they want me to go identify has a missing foot. That way I won't be going in for nothing. By the way, what's your name?"

"Stella."

"Welcome to New York, Stella," he says as he shakes my hand. "Come by again some time. Hopefully l won't be at the morgue."

It was lucky meeting Bob, not only because he was such a character, but also because he gave me a few good tips on finding an apartment. On with the sneakers and off to the streets. I could have let a real estate broker do the job, but in Manhattan, brokers charge 17 percent of the first year's rent. Besides, I wanted the experience of getting my very first Manhattan apartment rental lease all by myself.

As Bob had suggested, I jumped on anyone l saw with "Super"(intendent) embroidered on his overalls and carrying a bucket of paint. I was told to look for buildings with sheets down the stairs. This is a sign that workman-ship is taking place, and usually in a vacant apartment.

I see a brownstone on Ninth Avenue fitting this description. I march up the stairs and walk into a beautiful, newly renovated apartment where four workers are applying finishing touches.

"Who's the landlord of this building?" I ask.

They point at the supermarket across the road. I give them five bucks each to tell anyone else who marches up the stairs that the apart-ment is taken. I enter the supermarket.

"Hey asshole! I told you to move those

boxes of tuna fish. What are you waiting for? Islamic New Year?" yells someone from the other side of the supermarket.

This charming guy is Sidney and, as I soon find out, the landlord's son.

"I'm so tired and stressed out I could close up right now and it's only ten in the morning," he complains.

"Hi. My name's Stella. I want to rent the apartment across the road."

"You gotta talk to my father. He makes all the decisions. But he ain't gonna wanna talk with you anytime soon. He's in the hospital with my mother right now. She's got these kidney stones to deal with. Six in eighteen months! I wish I had as much luck with the lottery. Anyway, they're always having to make her pee 'em out. It's a real painful process," he says as he scrunches his face.

"How can I get in contact with him?" I ask.

"You can't. He don't let me give out his number. And he's hard to catch. Lives in Jersey. Tries to make it in on Thursdays. Anytime from seven in the morning."

It's seven o'clock on Thursday morning. I sit on a frozen turkey until four in the afternoon when Sidney's dad, Morty, finally arrives.

It's my first night in my new apartment. I just can't believe I'm here. I hear Frank Sinatra in my head singing *New York, New York.* I look out of my bedroom window. I see the Empire State Building on my right and pretend it's my personal night light. I see the hustle and bustle on Broadway and people hurrying along trying to make it to the theater on time. And although I can't see her, the Green Lady stands on Liberty Island and continues to smile. She came from somewhere else, too. Just like me. She's a lesson in resilience, a reminder to shape up or ship out. Well, I'm not going anywhere. I'm too much in love with this city. New York. A dream come true.